7 — 7 — 12

Waiting For Mr. Right

A Novel
by

Christopher J. Moore

Clairvoyant Books Edition October 2008

Christopher J. Moore 1971 –
Waiting For Mr. Right
ISBN 0-615-2120451300

Manufactured in the United States of America

Visit our web site at http://www.clairvoyantbooks.com

Acknowledgments

I hope that this story will make people think about the choices we all make in this thing called life.

This book is for my mother and father, Marzen and Thomas Moore, Jr., my wife Maricia, daughter Jordan, and son Xavier, my brother, Tiny, and his wife, Doris. I also want to thank my nieces, Marzen and Danielle, the Biggs family, and the Theards for their love and support. Without the support of my family and friends I could not have told this story. Also, a special thanks to all the people who took a chance on me and read and loved my first novel, "God's Child."

Finally, a personal thanks to Lyman Parrigin and Maricia Biggs for their edits and suggestions.

Christopher J. Moore has written one other novel, "God's Child," and numerous screenplays and teleplays.

Waiting For Mr. Right

 **ONE**

Ahh shit, here we go again, Dolores King thought as she sat on the edge of her bed, watching Brad stroll toward her. She knew exactly what was going to come out of his mouth. This had become a bad routine.

Dolores was beautiful and brown, with a shapely figure that accentuated her long legs. Her hormones were raging. She wanted it just as much as he did. They had been together for a little over a year, and now they were engaged. However, she was a thirty-two year old virgin who was waiting for marriage. She figured she waited this long, might as well wait eight more months.

But it was getting harder and harder for her not to have sex, Brad being tall, dark, and damn near gorgeous with a body that would make any woman wet with excitement. And Dolores was no exception.

She was an independent successful businesswoman, who was in love, and had compromised herself on a few things when it came to her relationship with Brad, but sex was not one of them. She even told him that she would change her last name, something she said she would never do, but because it seemed to mean so much to him she decided she would—well, at least for a little while. She figured that once they were married for a few years, she would change her name back, and keep the name that her father gave to her, Dolores LaToya King.

So there was Brad standing in front of her, with a towel wrapped around his waist. His rippling stomach muscles glistened from the shower. He exuded sexuality as he flung his damp dreads out of his face. He looked at her with sex infused eyes trying to seduce her, and it was working. Dolores sighed, feeling the temperature rise between her legs. But she remained strong.

She was also somewhat amused by the fact that, here she was thirty-two years old, in her prime, and a virgin with a sexy half-naked man standing in front of her, and not having passionate sex.

However, Dolores was no saint. She did everything short of intercourse. She often said that not having sex just seemed like the right thing to do, maybe because she was a daddy's girl, or maybe because of all of the different shit she could catch out there. But she would also say that if she knew that it was going to take this long to get married, she would have had sex a long time ago.

Dolores' parents raised her in the church. She went at least three times a week all the way up until she was sixteen, and it had an impact. When she went to college, she started to date, go to parties, and spread her wings a little bit. She went to UCLA and studied marketing. She felt UCLA was the perfect school for her. Being from Washington, DC, she got the space from her family she needed, and it was a way for her to be truly on her own for the first time in her life. She also knew that for the industry she would be going into, she couldn't be in a more perfect city.

So now here she was, sitting on her bed staring up at Brad, trying her best to resist him in all his splendor.

"Baby, I've been thinking," Brad said in his deep, smooth voice. He let out a sigh and sat on the edge of the bed. Dolores put down her glass of juice and crossed her beautiful brown legs, splitting her lavender silk robe in half. "I know you wanna wait until we get married, but now we're engaged; isn't that enough? I mean we're officially committed, right?"

"Baby, let's not have this discussion again."

"Why not?"

"Because. Look, we've waited this long. Let's just wait until we get married."

"This is ridiculous."

"It's just ridiculous to you, that's all." Brad's eyes narrowed. Dolores sensed that he was getting more agitated.

"Let's just change the subject, all right?" Dolores put her hand on his leg. Brad rolled his eyes. "Look, I promise when we get married, it will be worth it." Dolores smiled at Brad. He glared back at her, then got up and walked to the bedroom door. "Stop acting like that, okay?" Dolores exposed a slight smile, hoping to break the tension. Hands on hips, Brad returned a half smile of his own. She could see that he was struggling to hold back his frustration.

"All right," Brad said.

"Give me a real smile."

"You know it's just, I love you so much. And I will always love you, and to make love is the most beautiful thing in the world to do with someone that you love," Brad said.

"You don't think I have urges? I feel like I'm 'bout to explode here."

"Well, if you feel the same urges I feel, then just let it happen."

"I want to," Dolores said.

"Baby, I love you! Stop holding back." Brad strolled back toward her. The thought lingered in Dolores' mind as the man she loved approached her.

# TWO

Dolores woke up in her big bed wearing an expression of pure satisfaction. She turned over as if someone was in bed with her and grabbed the gold vibrator that lay next to her. She sighed and put the vibrator under her mattress.

She got up, strolled into the kitchen, and made a bowl of cereal and two pieces of toast. She sat at her dining room table and ate breakfast while reading the newspaper. After that, she ran the treadmill in the living room for forty-five minutes, while watching the news. When she finished, she jumped in the shower, shuffled through her expensive wardrobe of business suits, and took off for work. This was her daily routine, and she never wavered from it.

Dolores walked into a high-rise on Wilshire Boulevard. She went up to the nineteenth floor, where a huge sign read "Network Advertising Agency." Dolores strolled through the corridors making small talk, and telling random people good morning. She walked into her office. The plaque on her door read

"Director Of Marketing." She checked her messages then grabbed her coffee cup and headed to the break room. She went about her morning ritual, adding two packs of Equal and a dash of hazelnut creamer in her coffee. She gave it a quick stir. Tony Brooks strolled by and did a double take. He was medium built, handsome, dressed in an Italian suit. The epitome of confidence. Tony entered the coffee room, getting Dolores' attention. Dolores looked at Tony. Her distain was apparent under her fake smile.

"Oh hi," Dolores said.

"Hey," Tony said, preparing his coffee.

"You're up early."

"As are you," Tony said, with a sly smirk.

"Well, you know, I'm trying to get a head start. And you?" Dolores asked, with the most dishonest smile she could muster up.

"Oh, same here," Tony replied.

They continued to size each other up while stirring their coffee. "Uh hum," Tony said.

"Yep." Dolores walked out. Tony stood there for a second, then poured his coffee in the sink and walked out.

🆄 🆄 🆄 🆄

There were ten men and three women sitting around a conference table. At the head of the table was Bently, a heavyset man in his mid-fifties. He radiated authority, and it was clear that he was running the meeting. He was the man, and would often refer to himself as such. He would say, "Well, since I'm the man, we do it my way." He was a good boss that was definitely about his business.

On either side of him sat Dolores and Tony, waiting for the small talk to subside so the meeting could begin. Bently raised an open hand, the signal for everyone to quiet down. Dolores stood up and walked toward a chart that sat on an easel on the side of the room. She paused. "I think that this marketing scheme should be done over," she said. Her co-workers did not take this well. Many of them sighed harshly, shooting each other looks.

"What are you talking about? The marketing scheme is fine," one man shouted out.

"Look, we are competing against three products that always rank in the top ten. This is a crucial time for us. It's better to just take the time to create a new concept." There were sighs and murmurs throughout the room. Suddenly, Bently chimed in.

"What do you think, Tony?" Dolores cut her eyes at Bently, then focused on Tony. Tony and Dolores locked eyes for a moment. Tony took his time answering, showing that the wheels in his head were turning. Dolores sighed, putting a hand on her hip. He acted like the Godfather about to school his flunkies, which irritated Dolores.

"Well, we will lose money, but I think Dolores has a good point. The concept could be better," Tony said with his game face on, looking like he was figuring it all out on the spot. "And…"

"I think we need to focus on the longevity of this product, not the quick buck," Dolores chimed in.

"Dolores has a great point. It would be a shame, especially with as much work we've put into this product, to lose our targeted audience because of one bad spot," another man added. Dolores gave him a quick nod. Tony gestured with a finger getting everyone's attention. He went into deep thought, placing his index finger on his temple. He was smooth and deliberate, and Dolores hated him for it.

"Well, this is a new product so we need to be careful about what we're putting out there. I kind of planned on this, so I already started working on a couple of things concerning the marketing scheme," Tony said, sitting up more erect. Dolores stood frozen, grinding her teeth. If she had a gun, she would've shot him. "I'll make whatever adjustments this weekend, and it'll be ready on Monday."

"Well, it's my project. I'll do it," Dolores snapped.

"Dolores, just let Tony do it. Aren't you going to visit your parents in DC this weekend anyway?" Bently asked.

"I'll cancel it," Dolores replied.

"Let Tony handle it; you go see your parents," Bently said. Dolores gave Tony an evil glare. "Oh, by the way, I'd like to congratulate you on your engagement," Bently said, wearing a huge smile. This caught Dolores off guard. She looked at Bently, baffled. Everyone applauded, making Dolores feel extremely uncomfortable. Bently laughed a little. "Liz told me."

"Bout time," Tony said, wearing a smile. Dolores cut her eyes at Tony, and everyone laughed.

"Where's the ring?" Bently shouted. Dolores blushed.

"Brad's getting it sized."

Dolores received congratulations from her co-workers. She was smiling, but she was thinking about her account and how Tony positioned himself to save the day. She had been checkmated by Tony and everyone in the room knew it.

"There's nothing really for you to do around here today, so take the rest of the day off and go see that new fiancé of yours," Bently said with a grand smile.

ᗑᗖᗑᗖ

Dolores and her best friend, Liz, were having lunch in the company cafeteria. Liz was a thirty-one-year-old busty diva, very cute and a little heavy. Liz received an AA degree from West LA junior college not far from UCLA. And, being the outgoing, promiscuous young woman that she was, it was only natural that she was at every UCLA party. And that's how they met, double-teaming a cutie-pie on the dance floor.

Liz planned to go to UCLA when she was done at West LA. However, she got a job at UPS, started to make good money, and never looked back. Over the years Liz and Dolores remained the best of friends, supporting each other like sisters. So when Liz was laid off, Dolores got her a job as a receptionist at her company. The people there loved her, only problem she talked too damn much.

Dolores played with the chicken in her teriyaki bowl, pissed off. Liz sat there, guilt ridden. Her eyes wandered around the room, trying to avoid Dolores' eyes. She felt bad about telling Bently that Dolores was engaged. Dolores was a woman who liked to be prepared for everything and never get caught off guard.

"I have been stepped on for the last time. I can't believe he gave Tony control over my account."

"That's men for you; they'll get you every time."

"Girl, I feel like I'm 'bout to lose it. He actually had the nerve to tell me congratulations on getting engaged. Like he gives a damn."

"Hmm," Liz said as her eyes ran from Dolores'.

"Tony sittin' up there trying to act like he's been doing so much work."

"Everyone knows you two are fighting for Tom's job when he leaves. Don't worry about him."

"I can't stand Tony."

"Girl, go see your parents and forget about him."

"I can't believe I'm leaving that snake to finish my project!"

"Let him finish it; it's still your project."

Dolores thought about it for a moment, then let out a huge sigh. "Well, I'm about to go," she said, gathering her things.

"Where you going?"

"Bently gave me the rest of the day off. He called himself being nice. Anyway, I'm going over Brad's, so give me a call later."

"Why don't you just call me when you get home?"

Dolores gave Liz a look, knowing that Liz and Brad didn't approve of each other.

꒰ ꒱ ꒰ ꒱

Dolores drove her Ford Explorer down Wilshire Boulevard. She flipped from station to station trying to find something she liked. She got frustrated and turned it off. She picked up her cell phone and called Brad.

Brad answered with beads of sweat trickling down his face. He was breathing hard. "Hello?"

"Hey," Dolores said.

"Hey, babe."

"What are you doin'?"

"Nothing."

"Oh…"

"Are you on your cell phone?" Brad asked with an expression of concern.

"Actually, I'm right around the corner from your place." Fear spread across Brad's face as he stared at the half-naked woman who lay across his bed. Nina was a sexy petite, light-skinned black woman, with freckles and dreads. She sat there calm and placid, but her eyes tightened as she watched Brad squirm.

"Yeah, I'm about to stop at the store. You want something?" Brad didn't answer. "Brad, are you there?" Brad's mouth hung open, shifting around.

Nina sat calmly, watching Brad panic. Occasionally she glanced at the painted flowers on her fancy red fingernails.

"Yeah, I'm here," Brad said.

"Well, do you want anything?"

"Yeah, chips and a soda," Brad said panicking.

"What kind of soda?"

"Whatever you get." His eyes were wide and his heart beat fast. Dolores pulled up to the store, still on the phone. She walked into the store. "Well, let me go," Brad said, looking out of his window.

"Why don't you keep me company until I get there?"

"C'mon babe, let me go."

"Tell me you love me?"

"C'mon now. What are you doing?"

"I'm getting something to drink," Dolores said nonchalantly. Brad stared at Nina, who stared back at him with a look of disgust.

"Are you at the store now?"

"Yeah."

"I gotta go."

Brad hung up the phone. He scrambled around the room panicking while putting on his clothes. Nina sat there calmly. Brad looked at her, crazed. "Will you hurry up and put on your clothes!"

"Don't scream at me," she said in the calmest voice she could muster up, while her eyes stayed tight. Brad sighed.

"Look, I'm sorry, but please put on your fucking clothes."

Nina remained on the bed, calm and collected.

"Why don't you just tell her?

"What?"

"You heard me, just tell her." Nina's anger started to bubble. Brad looked like he was in a bad movie. He stood there totally outdone.

"Please don't do this to me," Brad said, his forehead tight like a fist.

Dolores paid for her things and headed out the door. She rushed to her car and zipped off, ready to vent to Brad about her day at work and how Tony stuck it to her again.

Dolores always felt that she was handicapped by being a woman in a male-dominated field. There were lots of women at her company, but the higher up she moved, the more women seemed to disappear. Dolores worked extremely long hours to prove that she was more dedicated and hard-working than her male counterparts.

Brad knew everything about her job; he knew who was gay, who was sleeping with who, and everyone's title. It was a constant soap opera.

Dolores drove fast, eager to deliver the latest installment.

Nina, only half dressed, watched Brad scramble around the room picking her clothes off the floor.

"All right. Hurry up and go," Brad said, holding her clothes.

"I gotta use the bathroom first," Nina said. She eased off the bed, snatched her clothes from Brad, and sashayed to the bathroom. Brad looked like he was losing his mind.

Dolores drove fast listening to house music, honking her horn, zipping in and out of traffic. She pounded the steering wheel to the beat of the music.

Brad stood by the bathroom door. "Come on now, I know you can use it faster than that!"

"Don't rush me!" Nina shouted.

"Why you doin' this to me?"

"If you shut up, maybe I can finish."

"Is this your idea of revenge or something?"

The door opened slowly and Nina strolled out.

"Where are my keys?" she said with an attitude.

"Right here!"

Nina rolled her eyes, snatched her keys, and walked to the front door.

"Hurry up, damn!" Brad shrieked.

Dolores chirped the alarm on her Explorer and headed up to Brad's apartment on the third floor. Nina passed her on the stairs wearing a mischievous smile and looking at Dolores like they were old friends. Dolores returned her smile, perplexed, and continued up the stairs. Brad was slow to open the door when she knocked. When he finally did, Dolores walked in and took off her coat, making herself at home. Brad was jumpy.

"Here's your stuff, babe." Dolores handed him a bag.

"Thanks," Brad said. For the first time Dolores noticed his strange behavior.

"What's wrong with you?"

"Nothing," Brad answered. He wiped a bead of sweat from his forehead. Dolores grabbed her jacket and headed to the bedroom. Brad's eyes widened. He rushed to Dolores, grabbing her jacket out of her hands. "Here, I'll do it!"

"I can put my own jacket up."

"No, no I got it." Brad hustled the jacket to his bedroom.

"What's wrong with you?" Dolores asked again.

"Nothing," Brad said from his bedroom.

Brad peeked his head out. "I have to take a shower."

"All right, but hurry up. I have to tell you about work," Dolores said.

Brad rushed to the bathroom. He took off his clothes and started to brush his teeth, when he noticed in the mirror a small hickey on the side of his neck. "Shit!"

Dolores turned on the television. And flopped down on the couch. As she did, she caught sight of a cigarette butt with lipstick on it resting on top of the television. Her eyes sharpened. Dolores eased off of the couch and picked up the cigarette butt. She scanned the living room then marched straight to the bedroom.

She looked around, then heard Brad turn on the shower. Acting like she was up against a shot clock with time running out, Dolores looked at the bed and quickly snatched back the covers, putting her nose to the sheets. She took in a big whiff.

Brad stood outside the shower, testing the temperature of the water. As he was about to step into the shower, he was grabbed by his arm. Dolores had a tight grip. She stared at him, searching for the truth. "What the hell you doin'?" Brad said.

"No, what the fuck have you been doin'?"

"What are you talking about?" Brad tried to hide his guilt while Dolores continued to stare at him.

"You know damn well what I'm talkin' about."

"Girl, you crazy." Brad tried to step into the shower, but Dolores pulled him back so he couldn't wash off the scent of the other woman, they both knew existed.

"Why you tryin' to get in the shower, Brad?" Brad gave a sheepish grin, trying to play it off.

"I don't know what you're talkin' about."

Dolores' eyes were glossy, and the steam around her face seemed to be coming from her vexed expression and not the shower.

"Just be a man and admit what you did."

"You're not gonna make me say something that didn't happen." Brad jerked back and forth. He shook his head and tried to get into the shower, but Dolores pulled him away. Brad grabbed her wrist, trying to get her to let go. "Stop acting stupid. Why are you acting like this!?"

"Okay, I'll stop."

"Damn!" Brad shouted. They took their hands off each other and stood face to face.

"Just do me one favor."

"What?!"

"Do me one favor, Brad."

"Will you leave me alone then?"

Dolores nodded yes. "Close your eyes."

"No. Stop acting stupid."

"No, I'm serious; close your eyes."

"This is so ridiculous." Brad sighed. "Fuck it, I'll close my eyes."

Dolores looked at Brad with repulsion. Brad looked at her with some hesitation, then closed his eyes. Suddenly, he heard the sound of Dolores, sniffing his penis. His eyes sprung open and he jumped back. "What the fuck are you doing?"

Dolores rose, disgusted. "You piece of shit."

"What are you talkin' about? Look, if you got something on your mind, then just say it and stop playin' games."

"Brad, I don't need you to say anything. Your dick just said it all," Dolores said in a calm voice, with heart-aching pain behind it. She tried to walk away, but Brad grabbed her arm. She snatched it away and stormed out of the bathroom.

"Dolores, Dolores, I'm sorry!" Brad slammed his fist against the wall, angry with himself.

Dolores stormed out of the building and into her truck. Brad came running out, wearing only a towel around his waist. Dolores quickly started the car and tried to pull away, but Brad jumped in front of the car. The Explorer came to a halt. Dolores' eyes grew narrow. The thought of running Brad over would be a delicious reality. Brad stood in front of her car, one hand on the hood, the other holding his towel. Their eyes were locked.

"Baby, come upstairs so we can talk about this."

"Get your ass from in front of my car."

"You're gonna have to run me over then."

"Don't tempt me."

"Please, baby, come back upstairs."

Dolores used her index finger to call him over. Brad gave a slight smile as he walked over to her. Dolores let her window down halfway, leaving just enough room for Brad's face. She looked at him with soft eyes. Her chest rose and fell at a much slower pace, showing Brad that she had calmed down.

"Brad, do me a favor?"

"Anything."

"Take the ring back. Don't get it sized or nothin', just get your money back for it. Because I could never, ever trust you again. Just stay out of my life." Brad's eyes fell. He knew she meant it and that she would never forgive him. Brad stepped back from the truck. Dolores looked straight ahead and sped off, leaving Brad standing alone in the street—his towel around his waist and his hand resting on his head. Suddenly Dolores' truck came to a screeching halt. She backed up. Brad sighed, hoping to be forgiven. He stepped up to her window to talk, but before he could get a word in she snatched his towel from around his waist, and sped off, leaving him ass naked in the middle of the street.

 **THREE**

Dolores moped around her house cleaning up. It was already spotless, but she worked on the small details. Washing clean windows, dusting every inch of her furniture, as if she wanted to get rid of Brad's DNA.

A box with Brad's things sat in the middle of the room. She taped it up and wrote his name and address on it. Then she dragged it to the front door, feeling like she was lugging a ton of bricks. She wondered how she let this happen. Until six hours ago her life was perfect. She had a perfect job, a perfect man, and a beautiful home. She made a nice living and so did Brad; together they were in the market for a house in the Hollywood Hills.

And Dolores knew exactly what kind of house she wanted: At least four bedrooms; one she would turn into an office for herself, another into a guest room, and another for when they had children. And most of all a city view and a pool. She would not compromise on any of those things.

But now her perfect life was over and her future was uncertain. It was not in her nature to forgive and forget. But, a part of her wished she could forgive Brad. Or maybe wished she never got off work early.

She felt weak. She had not eaten since lunch. The nerves in her stomach made her lose her appetite, and she had a pounding headache from crying for two hours straight when she first got home. She now knew what heartbreak felt like, not a schoolgirl crush, or a fling gone wrong, but to have someone you truly love break your heart.

There was a knock on the door. Dolores stared at it for a moment. She hoped it wasn't Brad. Her heart beat twice as fast. She headed for the door trying not to make a sound.

She looked through the peephole and saw Liz standing there looking worried. She unlocked the door and opened it. Liz extended her arms and gave Dolores a big hug. Liz looked like she wanted to cry too. "It's all right, girl," Liz said as they held each other tight.

Dolores and Liz sat on the floor all night, listening to jazz and drinking wine.

"That son of a bitch," Liz said, then chuckled. "So you used my dick sniffin' technique, huh?"

Dolores smiled, embarrassed.

"I can't believe I did that, but I had to be sure."

"Like I told many of my girls, if you wanna get to the bottom of it you gotta get your hands a little dirty. People criticize it, but that shit works."

Dolores rolled her eyes with a slight chuckle.

"So what are you gonna do?" Liz asked. Dolores thought about it for a moment.

"I don't know. You know, sometimes I feel like it's just a curse being the only, well you know, virgin in the world."

"Being a virgin has nothing to do with it. Well, it might." They both laughed. "Men, they're just animals, that's all, and Brad is the biggest one," Liz said with a smirk, but her eyes wore a subtle hurt behind them.

"I don't know; all my life I've wanted a family. You know, a husband, two kids, and a dog. Shit, I'm gettin' old."

"Girl, you not gettin' old; thirty-two is not old."

Dolores thought about what Liz said as she sipped her wine. "All night I've been thinking, if I wasn't trying to be this morally correct woman, and me and Brad had a sexual relationship like normal couples, would he have still cheated?"

"Hell, yes! Once a cheater, always a cheater," Liz snapped. Dolores took it in and sighed.

"I just don't know."

"Well, it's better that you find out that he's a dog now than after you married the jerk." Liz downed her wine. "I tried to tell you."

"I know."

"Girl, men are going to be bangin' down your door."

"Yeah, and then when they find out I'm not givin' up no booty, they gonna be bangin' on the door to get out." They both laughed. "I need to be looser like you."

"Fuck you," Liz said. They both laughed.

"You know what I'm talking about."

"What?"

"You know how you do it."

"Please. You act like I have em' passing each other at the door."

"Girl, ain't nothing wrong with it; you're just very sexually active."

"I ain't ashamed of it."

"I know that." Dolores laughed.

"I just like sex."

"Hmm, maybe that's what I need."

"Now, let's don't make any rash decisions," Liz said, looking amused.

Dolores thought for a moment.

"I guess I've waited this long for Mr. Right, hmm. Might as well hang in there."

"Just forget about that jerk and go see your parents."

"I guess I don't have a surprise for my parents after all."

Dolores grew pensive. She thought about how happy her parents would have been to hear that she was going to be married. She knew that no matter how much money she made or how high she climbed the corporate ladder, her parents would still believe that she was not happy. To them success and happiness are measured by having a husband and kids. A family. "Are you gonna spend the night?" Dolores asked.

"I might as well. You're gonna need a ride to the airport tomorrow anyway."

"All right, let me get some blankets." Dolores and Liz eased off the floor and went to the linen closet. Dolores handed Liz some blankets, and the two of them went to sleep.

FOUR

Dolores and Liz rushed through the airport. They made a scene as they called out to the flight attendant to hold on before closing the doors. Dolores gave Liz a quick hug and kiss on the cheek, and boarded the plane. Liz stood watching her best friend. She felt sorry for her because she knew the sacrifices that Dolores had made and how important finding a husband and starting a family was to her. She also knew how excited Dolores had been to be going home and giving her parents the good news. However, Liz could not help but smile, happy as hell that Dolores and Brad were no longer together.

Dolores sat by the window staring out at the clouds. A tear fell from her eye. She really didn't want to go to DC now that she was single. Too much pressure to move back home, find a good man, and start a family there. That's all her parents talked about every time she came to visit. They always believed she should have stayed in DC, and that being close to her family would inspire her to have one of her own. But Dolores had always known she needed to get away from what was familiar so she could find herself and become who she was meant to be, not what they wanted her to be.

When Dolores exited the airplane she saw her mother, Jackie, waiting in the terminal. Jackie wore glasses and looked like a school teacher. Then she saw her father, Lenny, looking like an intellectual as well. She crept up behind them and surprised them with a tap on the shoulders.

"Hey!" Dolores yelled, wearing a huge smile.

"Hey!!" Jackie and Lenny replied. They embraced. It was obvious they missed each other immensely.

回回回回

When Dolores, Jackie, and Lenny got home, the rest of Dolores' relatives greeted her with a surprise. Everyone was there: Uncle Charles, Lilly, Grandma, Carrie and her husband, Kevin, and cousin Steve the minister, white collar and all. They hugged Dolores one by one, making her feel at home and very loved.

They all sat down at the dining room table to an awesome spread. They had black-eyed peas, white rice, fried catfish, salad, and cornbread. A perfect opportunity for Dolores to deliver the good news. If she had any.

"Steve, do you mind blessing the food?" Lenny asked. He smiled at his daughter, beaming with pride.

"No not at all; I'd love to," Steve replied. He looked at his family with a smile, then bowed his head. The rest of the family lowered their heads. The table went silent.

"Dear Lord, I'd like for You to bless this food today, so that we may continue to serve the true word of God. Today, Lord, we have a lot to be thankful for. We would like to thank you, Lord, for bringing our Dolores back home safe and sound. We are an especially blessed family."

"Yes, Lord," Jackie said.

"We are a family that understands what family is all about. And on this day…"

"Mmm," Lenny added.

Steve continued without missing a beat.

"Oh, blessed God, to which there is none greater, make Dolores' stay a good one, and let her feel the love that this family feels for her, so that she knows how much she means to all of us. In the name of the Father, Son, and Holy Ghost, amen!"

"Amen!" everyone said in unison. They all raised their heads with big smiles, as if God himself prepared the food. Dolores was touched.

"Boy, back in my day we'd just say, bless this food and eat," Grandma said, with a straight face, shaking her head. The family laughed. "You don't need to go through all that. God knows what's in your heart," Grandma said, eager to dig in.

"Let's eat," Lenny said.

Dolores was glad to be home.

The clicking and clacking of silverware and plates went on until everyone was finished. No talking, just grunts, mumbles, expressing that the food was delicious. The one thing about Dolores' family, when it came to dinner the food was always so good that no one would say a word until they were done.

"Mom, the food was great," Dolores said. Everyone agreed with smiles of satisfaction.

"Thank ya' thank ya' thank ya'. You guys are all so kind," Jackie said, giving herself a pat on the back.

"It's so funny how you don't realize how much you miss home until you visit," Dolores said, looking at her first cousin Carrie. She loved Carrie. They grew up together and were extremely tight right up until Dolores went away to college. Carrie would come down to UCLA to visit when she could, which was usually a couple times a year. But after she graduated and got a job they grew apart.

"Look at you all grown an' stuff," Dolores said.

"Tryin' to be like my big cuz'," Carrie replied.

Dolores looked at Carrie. She was proud, admiring how she had grown into a beautiful woman.

"You're doing just fine," Dolores said. Carrie looked at Kevin, then at Dolores.

"I am, aren't I." Everyone laughed.

"Dolores, what's up with LA? Is it as bad as it seems out there?" Kevin asked.

"Not really; it just depends on the area you live in. Like out here."

"Nah, I think it's a little worse than out here. Those boys be doin' those drive-by shootings like it's nothin'," Uncle Charles said. "And get a record deal for it." Everyone laughed.

"You know how the media blows every black situation out of proportion," Lenny said.

"Actually, it's got so bad out here and in Los Angeles with the black-on-black crime, the media has tried to downplay it because of the heat from the black politicians," Lilly added.

"My baby's a journalist," Charlie said proudly. Carrie looked at Dolores and rolled her eyes.

"My daddy's so proud," Carrie said. Everyone chuckled, eyes darting back and forth.

"Yeah, but most of the time the media makes it seem like we have to dodge bullets every other day to get to work," Dolores said, laughing a bit.

"Well, when they do talk about it, maybe sometimes they do put a little too much on it," Lilly said.

"Of course they do, and that makes black people look so bad," Lenny said. Grandma sat there as the matriarch of the family, twisting her lips down.

"I say they should start giving these little gang-bangers the death penalty," Grandma declared.

"Oh, mom, that's not the solution," Jackie said.

"Yeah, two wrongs don't make a right," Lenny added.

"That's the problem—you guys are too damn Christianfied," Grandma shot back, waving her finger. Dolores laughed, then the others chuckled as well—except for Dolores' parents.

"Oh, mama. You're the one that taught me that killin' is wrong, no matter what," Jackie said.

"That was before these young punks were doin' drive-bys like cowards. Shootin' up the wrong folks and all," Grandma said.

"Ain't that the truth. Kids are doing it because they're underage and can get away with it," Carrie said.

"Their parents need to start bringing these kids up in church," Steve said.

"Amen to that," Jackie testified.

"Their parents need to whip they lil' bad asses," Grandma spit out. Most of the family gave a quiet laugh—even Steve the minister.

"Mom!" Jackie said.

"What?" Grandma said, shoulders shrugged.

 **FIVE**

Brad and his best friend, Rob, worked out in a Fitness gym. They both jogged on their treadmills. Rob struggled to keep pace, huffin' and puffin'. He was about forty pounds overweight, but handsome with a killer smile. He had a wife and two kids. He was definitely an influence on Brad when it came to settling down and wanting to start a family with Dolores.

They met at Universal Studios. And both were VPs at different production companies that had deals with the studio. They had gravitated to each other, being the only black men in their building.

They loved to talk about how unfair the business was and how they hated the fact that because they were black they were expected to only bring in black projects. And all of them comedies. Silly comedies that had no story but played like a long skit, filled with lowbrow humor that would insult any slightly mature black person's intelligence.

Brad picked up the pace. He looked intense. "Man, I really fucked up." He wiped the sweat from his forehead.

"You got that right; so what you gonna do?" Rob asked.

"I don't know. Maybe just give her some time."

"Man, you better get that girl back. A thirty-two-year-old virgin with a good job! Nigga, are you crazy?"

"Hey, I've been callin'. She ain't takin' my calls."

"Have you went over there yet?"

"Well, yeah. But she wouldn't answer."

"I suggest you stay on her. Make her forgive you."

"I don't know, Rob, I think it's over. Dolores, she's got trust issues already, so she's not gonna be able to let this go."

"Man, every woman has trust issues."

"Yeah, it sure seems that way."

"I mean, don't get me wrong; we're the cause of their issues." They both give a knowing chuckle. "But damn, man, you got to fight to get her back. She probably just wants to see whether you're gonna give up."

"You think so?"

"Hell, yeah!"

"What about Nina?"

"Fuck Nina! That bitch still lives with her parents."

Brad drove his car down the street. He looked at the clock on his dashboard. It was seven o'clock and he knew that Dolores should be home. If she wasn't, he would just wait for her. He had a key and was going to use it if he had to. Brad was going to work it out no matter what. He knew that deep in Dolores' heart, she wanted them to be together. She wanted to get married more than anything.

As he pulled up in front of Dolores' condo, he saw her Explorer in her parking space. He sat thinking about what to say to her when he saw her. He did a double take when he saw Liz's car parked nearby.

"Shit."

He decided to wait it out until Liz left.

After spending three hours in the car, Brad let out a huge sigh and marched up to Dolores' condo. He knocked on the door. There was no answer. He knocked again. Still nothing. He thought that maybe she and Liz left with one of their other friends, so he fished his keys out of his pocket. Just as he put the key into the door, it whipped open. Liz was staring at him like he was a criminal. Brad jumped back, startled. "Hey, I didn't know anyone was here."

Liz folded her arms, ready to block him from getting in. "Well, obviously that's not the case."

"Anyway, can you tell Dolores to come outside?"

"Nope."

"Liz, look, I ain't got time for your games. So tell Dolores to come out here," Brad said, raising his voice.

"First of all who you gettin' all agie with? And besides, fool, you should know she's gone to DC."

"You mean she still went?"

"That's right; she ain't studyin' you." She folded her arms. "Karma's a mothafucker."

Brad looked like he wanted to jump on her right there.

"Whatever, Liz. Just stay out of my business, all right?"

"Look, Dolores said it's over for real."

"Well I'll let her tell me that."

"Fine. Call her when she gets back. I'm going to sleep." Liz slammed the door in his face.

"Bitch!" Brad shouted.

"Whatever, nigga!" Liz shouted back. Brad heard Liz put the chain on the door. He was about to slam his fist against the door but stopped himself and stomped off.

SIX

Dolores and Carrie strolled through the mall window-shopping. This was their old stomping ground—from junior high all the way up until Dolores left for college. Carrie did a couple years at the local city college, but like Liz decided that college was not for her. So she got a job at FedEx; she made good money, traveled for free and had her own apartment. This was great for a nineteen-year-old girl. Especially when most of her friends were working at Mc Donald's or Burger King with no benefits and living at home with their parents.

Carrie was as sweet as a girl could be. And funny as all hell once you got to know her. She was also a great listener, and was the perfect person to give Dolores the comfort she needed. That non-judging, but keeping-it-real kind of feedback that she needed more than anything. Carrie was not going to tell Dolores what she wanted to hear, but what Carrie truly felt in her heart.

"Did you tell your mom and dad?" Carrie asked.

"No, I figure why ruin my visit out here."

"But they knew about him, right?"

"Yeah, but they didn't know we were thinking about gettin' married."

"Damn."

"Hell, I waited to tell them so I could surprise them in person."

"Men are just stupid," Carrie said.

"You should have seen the look on his face." Dolores imitated Brad's facial expression and Carrie rolled, laughing. "What, what?" Dolores said, mimicking Brad.

"Well, better you caught him now than after you married him."

"Yeah, that's what Liz said."

"How is Liz anyway?"

"She's doing good. Actually, she's a receptionist where I work."

"You need to bring her next time you come up; shoot, girlfriend had me rollin' last time she was here."

"Yeah, she's a wild one," Dolores said. They laughed. "So, how do you like the married life?"

"It's cool; it's hard at times, but it has its benefits."

"Like sex?"

"You know it," Carrie said, with a silly smirk on her face. They busted out in laughter, then Carrie stopped. "Are you still a virgin?"

Dolores was caught off guard, but her expression answered Carrie's question. "Damn, you are!"

"The way my luck has been goin', I feel like gettin' laid is exactly what I need." Carrie laughed. "Hey, you waited til' you got married, right?" Dolores asked, not knowing what her response would be.

"Yeah, sort of." They laughed. "But I think if I didn't get married when I did, I would have went ahead and did it anyway."

"I don't know; sometimes I question the whole "it's a sin to have premarital sex" thing," Dolores said.

"I think that it's just how we were raised, that's all," Carrie said. Dolores sighed, thinking about Brad and the great life they could have had.

"Sometimes I think I have to be crazy to be this old and still a virgin."

"If having sex before you get married is an unforgivable sin, then everyone's goin' to hell," Carrie said. Dolores chuckled.

"Hmm, except me. Shoot, I'll be the only one in heaven, all alone, and horny as hell." They laughed. "I've just always dreamed of being in love with the first person I made love to."

"Trust me, girl, sex can be way overrated." Carrie thought about it for a moment. "Or not."

That night Dolores and her parents hung out in the living room. She was tired and was debating whether she should tell them what had happened with Brad. Finally, she decided she just didn't feel like going there. She wanted her short time at her parents' home to be a pleasant one. She sipped her wine, bopping her head to the jazz her father had on. The music was soothing, bringing a smile to her face.

Lenny smiled at his baby girl. "I remember when your mother had you. We were so happy. Do you know that me and your mother tried for almost five years before we had you?" Lenny said, letting out a big yawn.

"The doctor told us that it was not likely for me to get pregnant. He said that my eggs weren't producing correctly or something like that," Jackie added, sipping her wine.

"So you mean I'm like a miracle?" Dolores asked, smiling from ear to ear. They all laughed.

"Exactly," Lenny said, as he yawned again.

"I missed you guys so much."

"We missed you, too," Jackie said.

"Mom, how old were you guys when you got married?"

"I was nineteen and your dad was twenty-one."

"Wow." Dolores thought about Brad and how one mistake ended their life together. Lenny was nodding off, his mouth wide open.

"Being in love is a special thing. Something that's more important than any amount of money, job or anything—and you remember that," Jackie said.

"Being married isn't as easy as you and dad make it seem." Lenny had his head back and mouth wide open, snoring.

"It is. You just have to find the right person. And hopefully he'll be your best friend." Lenny snored louder. Dolores and Jackie looked at him amused.

"It's getting late," Jackie said, taking a final sip of her wine.

"Yeah."

"Wake up, let's go to bed," Jackie said to Lenny. She shook him awake.

"What, what, I'm not asleep," Lenny said, eyes barely open.

"Lenny!" Jackie said, shaking him some more.

"Huh, oh, what? I told you I'm not asleep."

"Whatever; let's go." Jackie pulled Lenny up off of the couch.

Dolores smiled at her parents. They had stood the test of time and their relationship was stronger than ever. Jackie turned back to Dolores. "Good night. Oh, don't forget to turn off the music."

ꍾ ꍾ ꍾ ꍾ

Dolores hugged and kissed her mother and father, then boarded the plane. She stared out the window as the plane took off. She wondered what her life would be like if she wasn't so focused on her career and moving up the corporate ladder. And why Brad cheated on her in the first place, and was she partly to blame. Then she thought, maybe all men are just full of shit. She sighed, then a mischievous grin spread across her face and she laughed out loud.

SEVEN

Nina knocked on Brad's door. He cracked the door open, half asleep. Nina was dressed casual, wearing a baseball cap with the visor down low.

"Hey, what's up?" Brad asked, clearing his throat, slightly irritated.

"Nothin'. I just wanted to see you."

"Damn, you don't know how to use a phone?" Brad remained behind the cracked door.

"Yeah, but I figured I'd just drop by. Move out the way." Nina pushed past Brad and walked inside. Brad closed the door and went to the kitchen to get a glass of water.

"Look, Nina, I need some time to think about all this."

"Think about what? She dumped you."

"Yeah, but I still want us to get back together."

"Why?" Nina took off her hat and inched over to Brad, trying to seduce him with her eyes and her hips. Brad looked her up and down as she moved closer.

"She could never make you happy the way I can. Hell, you don't even know her. She doesn't know your body the way I do. She doesn't know what you like. Brad, it all happened for a reason. We were meant to be together. C'mon baby, you know I'm right." Brad sighed, then took a sip of his water.

"I don't know what's right. What I do know is that I love Dolores." Nina was right up on Brad. She kissed him on the lips softly.

"Stop frontin'; you know you can't resist me." She kissed him again. Her eyes were closed but his were open, watching her closely. Then his eyes slowly closed as they continued to kiss. Brad suddenly pushed her off of him.

"You gotta go."

"What do you mean, gotta go?"

"I mean you gotta leave." Brad grabbed her and strong armed her out the front door. "Bye, Nina." He closed the door in her face hard.

"Brad, I know you not gonna just leave me out here!" she shouted. "Brad!"

EIGHT

Dolores landed in LA wearing a huge smile. She strolled through the airport like a woman on a mission, and caught a cab. The cab driver and Dolores exchanged glances in the rearview mirror. He could tell something was going on in her mind.

"Everything okay?"

"Yeah; actually, wait a minute. Take me to West Hollywood."

"No problem."

The cab pulled up in front of Liz's apartment building. Dolores told the driver to wait and ran into the building. She strolled up to Liz's door and knocked. Liz answered it in her nightgown, her hair in rollers.

"Hey!" Liz said. Dolores gave her a hug, but didn't come in.

"What's up, girl," Dolores said, glowing.

"Well, come in," Liz replied, looking at her strangely.

"No, I can't; my cab's waiting."

"Well, what's up?" Liz asked.

Dolores hesitated.

"I need to get laid," Dolores said, with hands on hips like a cheerleader after a great cheer.

"What!?" Liz busted out in laughter.

"What?"

"Oh, you're serious?"

"Yeah, I'm serious."

"Well, what do you want me to do?" Liz asked, tickled.

"Help me!"

"What am I, a pimp?"

Dolores gave a little laugh.

"No, you're not a pimp. I just want us to go to some clubs where there's some, men."

"Since when did I become the expert on finding men?"

"Please, girl; you go through more men than I go through clothes."

"Is that right?"

"That's right! Look, if I was looking for a husband, you know I wouldn't have come to you." Dolores had a big smile on her face and a look that said are you going to help me or not? Dolores started to laugh. "I'm just looking for sex."

Liz stood staring like Dolores was absolutely out of her mind. Dolores gave a little chuckle. "Your department." They looked at each other wearing huge grins.

"Come pick me up around eleven," Liz said matter of factly. "With your crazy ass."

"I knew you wouldn't let me down."

"All right. See you later." Liz shook her head, outdone. As Dolores walked away, Liz yelled out, "About time!"

NINE

Dolores sat at the bar listening to a man with a cowboy hat, thick Texas accent, tight jeans tucked in his red, white, and blue cowboy boots.

"I ain't gonna front. I'm 35 years old and I live with my mama, but my room's clean and I'm a fun guy."

Dolores stared at him with a blank expression.

Another man on the stool on the other side of her looked like a pimp. Purple silk suit, purple hat, pink shirt, and purple alligator shoes. He squinted, rotating his eyebrows back and forth, as if he was trying to hypnotize Dolores. She stared back at him, trying her best not to laugh.

"Look, baby, I don't have time for da' yakty yak. Why don't you just come to my place, let me lay you down on my bear-skin rug and gently wax…"

Dolores quickly put up her hand.

"Stop. Just stop." The pimp stopped, baffled, not understanding how she could resist him. She stared at him like he had a piece of shit growing out of his face.

An average-looking man with a nice smile sat at the bar wearing an Armani suit and a Rolex. Dolores smiled back at him, noticing how well he was put together.

"I'm out here on business but I'll be leaving tomorrow, so I thought I might get out my last night." Dolores was interested, then noticed he was scratching his crotch. She turned away, disgusted. He got the picture and strolled off, still scratching.

Liz pranced off the dance floor to the beat of the music and sat next to Dolores. Dolores looked totally outdone. Liz was amused.

"So how's pussy tryouts?"

"Ugh," Dolores said, sickened but laughing.

Dolores watched the different people around the club waving at Liz, who was obviously a regular. The bartender handed them their drinks.

"What's up, Liz? This is from those gentlemen behind you," the bartender said, wearing a smile. Liz and Dolores looked at the table behind them and saw three rough-looking characters.

"How's it goin'? Hey James, Larry. Who's your friend?" Liz said looking at the guy she didn't know. He was handsome with an edge to him.

"This is Henry," James said, wearing a charming smile.

"Hey," Henry said.

Liz smiled. "He's kinda cute," she said to James.

"I thought I was the only one for you!" Larry said, putting his hands over his heart.

"Baby, you know you are," Liz answered, with a puppydog expression. Dolores was looking straight ahead, sipping her drink with a big grin on her face.

"Damn girl, who don't you know in here?"

"That fine ass-man over there." Liz pointed to a man at the end of the bar. He noticed Liz pointing at him and waved back smoothly with one eyebrow raised. She waved back.

"Damn," Liz and Dolores said in unison.

"I'll meet you on the dance floor," Liz said. She eased off of the stool, adjusted her boobs, and strolled over to the man at the end of the bar. They exchanged a few words and headed to the dance floor.

"That girl is too much," Dolores said to herself, watching Liz's butt jiggle all the way to the dance floor.

Dolores was becoming more and more bored when she noticed Trey White. He walked in like he owned the place. He was tall and muscular, with broad shoulders. His skin was like dark chocolate, smooth with a deep shine. And he had a beautiful smile. Dolores was attracted to him like no man since Brad. But this attraction was very different. She looked at Brad like husband material. But this attraction was a stinging lust, and her mind was filled with dirty, nasty thoughts. She said to herself, If you're gonna go out, he would be a great way to do it.

Trey scanned the club like the king of the jungle looking for his next meal. He zeroed in on Dolores. But as he headed toward Dolores, Liz snatched her by the arm.

"Come here, I got somebody for you to meet," she said, dragging Dolores across the dance floor.

"Damn, girl!"

"C'mon." Liz continued to pull Dolores while she and Trey stared at each other.

Trey stepped up to the bar, looking at some of the other women who passed by. The bartender approached him.

"What's up, Trey?"

Trey soon enough found himself on the dance floor to get his groove on. As he started to dance he noticed that he was dancing next to Dolores. He stared at her, licking his lips. He liked the way she moved, even though she seemed a little out of practice. He thought it was cute. The woman dancing with Trey saw him looking at Dolores, but just smiled. She knew how Trey was—he was a true ladies man and wasn't ashamed of it.

Dolores saw him watching her. They smiled at each other. Her smile let him know that she was open to whatever. But Liz saw Dolores flirting with Trey, who she had spent time with on a few occasions herself. She grabbed Dolores and marched her into the ladies room.

Dolores stared at Liz, who was fixing her makeup. "What the hell is wrong with you?" Dolores said confused.

"So what do you think of Roy?" Liz asked, checking her lipstick.

"He's all right," Dolores answered.

"Well forget about Trey."

"Who's Trey?"

"The buff brotha' you was checkin' out."

"Do you work here or somethin'?" They busted out laughing.

"Look, I know Trey. Matter fact, I know him well."

"Are you serious?"

"Yeah. We went out a couple of times, but that was a while ago."

Dolores paused for a moment. "Was he good?"

"Huh?"

"You heard me."

A smile crept across Liz's face. "Yeah, yeah, he was all right. C'mon."

"Well introduce me to him... if you don't mind," Dolores said, as giddy as a schoolgirl with a crush. Liz stood looking at Dolores, amused.

"He's a dog."

"Maybe that's what I need. A dog!"

"Well, what about Roy?"

"Not my type."

Liz hesitated for a moment.

"All right, all right, I'll introduce you." They exchanged smiles and headed back to the dance floor.

They both scanned the place, looking for Trey. "I don't see him," Liz said, hoping he had gone.

"You think he left?"

"With Trey, who knows."

Eric and Roy—the two brothas they were dancing with—strolled toward them, smiling.

"Girl, I'm 'bout ready to go," Dolores said, trying her best not to move her lips.

"Yeah, me too."

"So what's up, ladies?" Eric asked.

"Nothing, but I think we're gonna go home," Liz said, charming as ever.

"I thought we were gonna get something to eat afterwards." Roy said, looking a little desperate.

"Well, I'm kinda tired so we're gonna go home," Dolores said, letting out a fake yawn.

"Yeah, we have to go to work early tomorrow," Liz added.

"Hey, well that's cool," Eric said, disappointed.

"Maybe we can do something tomorrow then," Roy said.

"Yeah maybe so. Eric, you got my number, right?" Liz asked.

"I got it."

The guys looked like they were starving in a restaurant, and the waiter took back their food.

"All right, see you guys later," Dolores said, sensing their desperation.

"Bye, boys," Liz said, still flirting, making her exit that much more painful for Eric and Roy.

"Bye," the fellas said, as the ladies strolled out of the club, catching the eye of every man as they did.

TEN

"Barry, I don't know what happened. But look, we'll have it on time." Dolores paused. "I give you my word." She listened, becoming irritated. "Look, when I see Tony we'll talk about it and I'll get right back to you." She paused again. "Yes, Bently approved it. All right?" Liz walked into Dolores' office, and Dolores signaled her to have a seat. "Yeah, Barry, all right. Yes. For the last time, I put it in your box." She took a final pause. "Talk to you later." Dolores looked at Liz, exhausted. "Have you seen Tony?"

"I saw him earlier."

"I think that bastard's sabotaging my work."

"What are you talking about?"

"I left some forms for Barry to sign, and he said they weren't in his box."

"Well, just ask Tony."

"What do you think—that he's just going to up and say, 'Yeah, Dolores, I took your forms so you would look incompetent'? Nope," she barked, as she threw her hands in the air.

"I gotta get back to my desk," Liz said. She strolled out, thinking about her own drama. She didn't have time for Dolores'.

◫◪◫◪

The knock on the door sounded like a police officer paying a visit. Tony's eyes shot up. "Come in." Dolores stepped into his office smiling, but the smile didn't hide her anger.

"You got a minute?"

"Sure," Tony said, doing his best to not make eye contact.

"So, how's work?" Dolores asked. Tony read her expression.

"It's fine. Is everything okay?" Tony asked.

"Actually things are pretty far from okay."

"Well, if I can help just let me know."

"Actually there is something that you can do."

"Name it."

"Stop sabotaging my work, you back-stabbing son-of-a-bitch!" Dolores yelled.

"What are you talkin' about?"

"You know what I'm talkin' about." Dolores stared at Tony as if she could see straight through his lying eyes.

"Look, I really don't know what you're talking about."

Dolores stood there reading his face like a short story.

"Just leave my work alone, Tony. What you're doing is not fair, and it's not right." Dolores stormed out and slammed the door shut.

◻ ◻ ◻ ◻

A dozen employees sat at the conference table talking. Bently looked on disappointed. Dolores and Tony sat on either side of him. Guilt on one side and anger on the other.

"All right, all right, let's get started," Bently said. Everyone got quiet.

"First, new business. I'd like to thank Tony for finding Dolores' packet. Dolores, I don't know what happened, but we can't have screwups like that." Dolores avoided looking at Bently while steam rose from her head. Bently took a deep breath. "What happened?"

"I put the packet in Barry's box at three o'clock," Dolores said, trying to keep her composure.

"He said it wasn't there," Bently replied.

"What do you want me to say?" Dolores asked, shooting Tony a quick look.

"Just that sometimes you need to double-check things. Lucky for us, Tony found it in Linda's box above Barry's. It's just a good thing he caught it in time."

"All right," Dolores said, as she threw Tony a final look. Tony stared straight ahead, feeling the heat on the side of his face.

▣ ▣ ▣ ▣

Dolores was watching television when the doorbell rang. She walked to the door like she had a fifty-pound weight on her back. "Who is it?"

"It's me, girl," Liz answered. Dolores opened the door and Liz strolled in, dressed in a beautiful black gown. "How come you not ready?"

"I'm not in the mood to be dealing with Tony or Bently."

"Well, damn, how come you didn't call and tell me?"

"I just changed my mind."

"I came all this way over here—you're goin'."

"Just go without me."

"Hell no! Maybe you'll meet a guy."

"Whatever."

"Whatever happened to," Liz mimicked Dolores. "I wanna get laid, Liz, take me out Liz?" Dolores rolled her eyes and headed to her bedroom.

"Will you shut up."

"Where you goin'?"

"I'm going to get dressed." Dolores shot a fake smile and Liz mirrored it.

ꔷꔷꔷ

Dolores and Liz entered the ballroom at the Hilton looking beautiful. They found their co-workers at a large table. Dolores smiled, but she did not want to be there. Bently was wearing a big smile, enjoying himself. He sipped his drink while cracking jokes. He was a completely different person when he was in the social scene. He would laugh and joke about people's work ethic, and sometimes even make fun of himself.

"Hey, Dolores. Liz," Bently said, laughing at a joke he just told. Everyone at the table was laughing. Bently was funny, but he wasn't that funny.

"Hi. Hi, everyone," Liz said with a wave.

"Hello, Bently. Hey, everybody," Dolores said, with a slight attitude. Dolores waved at everyone. She leaned over to Liz. "I don't know why I let you talk me into coming," she whispered.

"You need to do some schmoozin' for that promotion," Liz whispered back. "Oh God, look who just walked through the door."

Tony strolled in looking very handsome. His wife Mary was on his arm. She was petite and beautiful and exuded an aura of innocence. She wore a six-carat tennis bracelet and a three-carat diamond wedding ring. She made sure her bracelet and wedding ring were always exposed, constantly waving them in people's faces.

"Don't sweat him, girl," Liz said.

"Oh I'm not. He's such a worm."

"He looks kinda good, though," Liz said. Tony and Mary approached their table. Tony's eyes once again avoided Dolores'.

"Hello, everyone. You guys all know my wife, Mary?"

"Of course," Bently said, rising and kissing Mary's hand.

As the night went on, Dolores got restless. She scanned the ballroom, noticing that everyone seemed to be in a relationship. This not only depressed her, it also made her angry—and sad that she and Brad broke up. She thought, maybe she should forgive him and get back together just for the sake of not being alone. Hell, nobody's perfect, and after all Brad is just a man. Not Superman, but a man. Liz once told her that all men are dogs, and that a woman should just strive to get a good one. She didn't believe that when Liz told her, but now she felt like Liz might have been on to something.

"Excuse me, ma'am, would you like something to drink?" the waiter asked with a smile. Dolores snapped out of her trance. She looked up at him with soft eyes.

"No, I'm about to leave."

The waiter smiled and headed off. Dolores got up and walked over to Liz, who was dancing slow and close with a tall man, eyes locked. They looked like a couple the way they held each other, but that was just Liz's style. She was always very comfortable around men. Liz broke eye contact as Dolores stepped to her.

"Hey."

"What's up?" Liz asked, beaming.

"I'm about to catch a cab and go home."

"Look, just give me a couple minutes and we can go," Liz said, disappointed.

"No, no, you enjoy yourself. I kinda wanna take a ride by myself, clear my head."

"You sure?" Liz asked, checking to see if Dolores was all right.

"Yeah."

"All right, girl, be careful."

"All right. 'Ey—did you bring your phone? I forgot mine."

"It's in the car."

"I gotta find a phone so I can call a cab."

"All right. Call me tomorrow so we can work on that…" Liz paused and looked at her dance partner. "That problem of yours." Her smile was comical. Dolores returned the smile with a chuckle.

"All right," Dolores said and headed off.

Dolores found a bank of phones against the wall, separated by tall plants. As she began to dial. She was thrown off by the sound of familiar voices, arguing in a hushed tone. She was about to try to see who it was, but someone answered the phone.

"Hi. Em', I need to be picked up in front of the Hilton Hotel in Studio City. Yes, my name's Miss King. Okay, I'll be out front." Just then Dolores heard her name amongst the arguing. She froze, then picked up the phone again and pretended to have a conversation. She peeked through the huge plant that separated them, and saw Mary and Tony.

"Enough's, enough," Tony said, in a stern tone.

"What are you talking about? She doesn't care about your job. Why should you care about hers?" Mary shot back.

Dolores wanted to jump over the plant and choke Mary out right there.

"Look, baby, I just want you to get what you deserve, that's all," Mary said, caressing Tony's face.

"I don't want Dolores to lose her job over it." Tony moved her hand from his face.

"Stop being so damn soft!" Mary fired back.

"I'm not being soft."

"Just help her lose a couple more important documents, then…"

"I hate this," Tony said, wiping the sweat off of his forehead. Dolores sympathized with Tony for a moment, but the moment passed—she was too repulsed to give a damn. She felt like she was out of her body, watching two people she disliked decide her fate.

"I am so tired of having to tell you what to do to be successful. Why can't you do something on your own for once? Be a man, for God sakes."

Tony stood there, pathetic.

"I am a man," Tony said.

"Well act like it."

Mary stomped off. Tony stood there looking like he wanted to kick her in that beautiful ass that he fell in love with. But instead he just hung his head and followed her, looking like a child that just got his butt whipped.

Dolores was already thinking about her next move.

ELEVEN

Dolores thought about going to Bently, but she might look like she was just trying to blame someone else for her mistake. She thought about calling Tony out in a meeting so everyone could watch his reaction, and see him for the lying snake he was.

She phoned Liz. She sat on the couch venting.

"I could not believe what I was hearing," Dolores said, trying to control her rage.

"Are you serious?"

"Girl, the boy looked pathetic."

"So what are you gonna do?"

"Hey, two can play that game."

"Men are so scandalous," Liz said.

"You damn right they are."

"Damn. They never cease to amaze me!" Liz paused. "Are we still goin' out?"

"Girl, did you just hear what I said?"

"Yeah, but what does that have to do with us goin' out?"

"You are so simple."

"So, are you still goin' out? That's what's important, right? Stay focused. Don't let this fool get you off track."

"Yeah, I guess," Dolores said, reluctant.

"That's my girl."

"Come get me around ten, 'cause I got a lot of work to do tonight."

"All right."

TWELVE

Brad was sprawled out on the sofa in his underwear watching television. He hadn't showered or shaved in a week. He barely moved when he heard a knock on the door. He wasn't expecting anyone. He figured it was Nina popping over, even though he had told her on too many occasions not to just drop by. He was not in the mood. He snatched the door open, ready to tear in to... But it was Rob and their friend Zach, drunk, laughing like kids on a playground.

Zach was the friend that everyone's girlfriend or wife hated. He was definitely a bad influence on anyone trying to nurture a relationship. He was funny but unruly. Women either loved him or hated him instantly.

Zach and Brad grew up together and played basketball in high school. Zach was a ladies man, but he treated women like they owed him money.

"What the hell are you doin' here?" Brad asked, irritated. "I told you guys I don't wanna go out."

"Just shut up, bitch, and put on your clothes," Zach said, still laughing from something Rob told him on the way to the door.

"I'm not going."

"Yes you are," Zach said.

"I told you we shouldn't have come. Shit, I don't get too many nights away from the wife. And I don't want this dude messin' up my night," Rob said.

"He won't. Now put on some clothes and shave that shit off of your face," Zach said to Brad like he was his father.

"I told you I'm not going."

"Look man, this is exactly what you need. Shit. You gotta get your mind off that broad," Zach said.

"Dude, do you understand English!?" Brad shouted.

⊔⊓⊔⊓

Brad sat sullen in the back of Zach's Chevy Impala. Zach shoved the bottle of Hennesey in Brad's face. "Now just drink." Brad grabbed the bottle. His friends were right—Hennesey was the remedy for his problems. At least for tonight. He took two big swallows. He gazed at the bottle like they were old friends.

"All right, fuckers, let's get to the club," Brad said, with pure determination in his eyes.

"That's my boy," Zach said, smiling like the devil himself.

"Just don't get too wasted," Rob said.

"I just lost my fiancée. Shit, I got nothing to lose. Just get me to the damn club."

"See, that's the nigga that I know and love," Zach said, drinking out of his own personal flask with his initials Z.H. engraved on it.

When they pulled up in front of the nightclub, a line of people stood out front waiting. The men looked stylish and the women looked sexy. "Now that's what I'm talking about," Zach said, biting at the ladies as if he was taking a chunk out of them.

"Brad, you okay back there?" Rob asked.

"Yeah, I'm cool." Brad took another swig from the bottle.

 **THIRTEEN**

Loud music pounded away as Dolores and Liz strolled in a nightclub. They both showed just enough cleavage to get the fellas' attention, but not so much that a guy would think that if his rap didn't work, he could just pay her.

Guys checked them out as they strolled to the bar. Dolores liked the attention. Liz looked at her, smiling. "Girl, what's come over you?" Liz asked.

"Nothing. Just trying to figure how I'm gonna get back at Tony, that's all."

"Can we stop talkin' about work and find some men?"

"All right," Dolores said, with a smirk.

Dolores and Liz found a table and a waiter approached them.

"How you ladies doin'? Can I get you something?" The waiter looked like an aspiring model working his day job, enjoying the perks of serving beautiful women. Dolores and Liz smiled.

"Yes, uh, I'll have a Long Island Ice Tea," Dolores answered, anxious to get some alcohol in her bloodstream. Liz looked the waiter up and down, tickled by his good looks.

"And I'll have a Gin and Tonic."

Dolores and Liz scanned the room for eligible men. The waiter returned with their drinks in a flash, wearing a huge smile, which he directed at Dolores. Dolores took a big swallow of her drink. "Girl, be careful with them Long Island Ice Tea's," Liz said.

"Thanks for your concern, but I got this." She took another gulp.

As the girls got tipsy, they found themselves having more and more fun. They accepted an invitation to dance from David and Mark and were having a ball. Best of all, Dolores seemed to forget all about her troubles at work. Thanks to Mr. Long Island.

Dolores and David finally left the dance floor and headed to the bar. David was squat with a bald fade and glasses. He was the total opposite of Brad, and yet Dolores was still attracted to him. She thought he was cute, and liked his smile. It also seemed like he knew how to treat a lady. To Dolores, there was nothing more attractive than that.

David looked like he hit the jackpot, eyeing everything about Dolores from her pretty hair to her manicured toes.

"Is this your first time here?" David asked.

"Yep," Dolores replied.

"So, do you like it?"

"Yeah, it's cool."

"Do you live around here?"

"Huh?" Dolores said, leaning in, trying to hear him over the music.

"Do you live around here?" David asked again, raising his voice.

"Oh yeah, I live in the Hollywood area."

"That's cool..."

Dolores cut him short, signaling the waiter.

"Same?" the waiter asked.

"Yes." Dolores replied.

"What are you drinking?"

"Long Island Ice Tea."

"Are they good?"

"Real good."

The waiter returned and handed Dolores her drink. She let out a huge sigh before taking a sip. "It's good. Trust me."

"Uh, could you get me one of those?" David asked the waiter. The waiter shot David a look like he stole something.

"Sure," the waiter said.

"Here, taste mine," Dolores said.

"Let me see." David took a sip of Dolores' drink and smiled. The waiter returned with David's drink and dead eyes. David noticed the waiter's expression.

"Here you go," the waiter said.

"Thank you." David laughed it off. They both gave a little laugh as the waiter strolled off. "I think you got a fan." Dolores turned to watch Liz and Mark slow dance.

Mark was tall and good looking. Liz stared up at him, searching for the words that would make her feel good enough to want to take him to a hotel and have sex. Mark stared down at her. She knew that he was feeling her. If not from his eyes, then from his erection. He pressed it against her stomach, not embarrassed at all by it. It was his way of letting her know what he was working with. Liz didn't pay it any mind—this wasn't the first time she had a hard dick pressed against her stomach, and she knew that it wouldn't be the last.

"You're so tall."

"I'm not that tall."

"How tall are you?"

"Six three."

"And you don't think that's tall?"

"I used to play basketball, and six three isn't that tall for basketball."

"I like tall men."

"And I like short women."

"I'm not short."

"Oh, I mean tall women," Mark said playfully.

"Now you know I'm not tall, either."

"Well, beautiful women."

"Aww, that's sweet." They stared into each other's eyes.

"C'mon, let's go see how our friends are doing," Mark said with a charming smile.

They strolled over to Dolores and David. Liz wore a smile, seeing Dolores flirting with David. "So what's up?"

"Nothin' girl," Dolores said.

Liz did a double take, realizing that Dolores was drunk.

"What are you guys gonna do after this?" Mark asked, a little anxious.

"Go home, all alone." Dolores looked at David like she wanted to have sex with him right there. Mark and David exchanged a glance.

"Well, let's all get out of here and do something," Mark said.

"We can go to my house," Dolores said matter of factly. Liz shot Dolores a surprised look.

"No, let's go somewhere else, like the beach," Liz said.

"Oh, that'll be fun," Dolores said. The guys looked at each other with a smile.

"Cool!" David and Mark said at the same time. Liz leaned close to Dolores, so only she could hear.

"Go to your house? Girl, we don't know these fools like that," Liz said. Dolores chuckled, still staring at David.

# FOURTEEN

The fellas danced like they had something to prove. Brad sweated profusely, flirting with the woman in front of him. He looked like he hadn't been out in a long time.

His boys knew that this was exactly what Brad needed to get his mind off Dolores: dancing with a beautiful woman with a handful of ass. Brad moved in closer and closer on the cutie. She stepped back, giving him the "it's cool" but back up off a sista' look. He smiled, then grabbed her around her waist and pulled her into him. She slowly pushed him off of her, but continued to dance with him. Brad backed off for a few seconds, then grabbed her by the waist and pulled her in once again. He held her tightly, grabbing her ass now with both hands, squeezing it like he was trying to cut off her circulation. She pushed him away hard, and stomped off. Brad's eyes lit up. He rushed through the crowd like a man possessed, knocking people out of his way. He caught up with her and grabbed her by the arm.

"Fool, are you out of your mind?!" the cutie snapped.

"What!" Brad said, looking drunk.

She pulled free and turned to walk away. Brad quickly snatched her by the arm again. By this time people were looking at the commotion. She tried to get loose, but Brad's grip was too tight around the girl's tiny wrist.

"What the hell is your problem?!" Brad shouted over the loud music.

"Get off of me!!" she yelled back.

"Well fuck you, then!"

"No, fuck you!" She swung at him with her free hand, smacking him across the face. Brad let go and raised a fist. The girl stood there undaunted. "What, you gonna hit me mothafucka? Well, swing!" The petite cutie's tiny manicured fist was balled up, ready to strike him back. He was taken aback by the young brave girl. Brad stood there frozen, realizing that the people at the club were staring at him like he was some kind of maniac. Suddenly, Rob grabbed him by the arm. Brad was startled, and almost punched Rob out with the fist meant for the young woman.

Rob marched him to the restroom. Zach saw the drama from afar and headed to the restroom as well.

"What the fuck is your problem, man?!" Rob shouted. He could not believe what he just saw.

"Man, that bitch hit me!"

"Dude, that's because yo' ass was manhandling her. Shit, I would of hit yo' ass, too," Rob said.

"I wasn't manhandling her."

"Dude, you're trippin'!" Rob said. Brad paced the floor like a caged lion. His fist was clenched like he was ready to fight. And his eyes were red from alcohol.

"Fuck you! Shit, I didn't ask to come out to this mothafucka!" Brad punched the restroom mirror, shattering it. Zach ran into the restroom and saw the glass all over the floor— and Brad's bloody fist.

"Brad, you all right?" Zach asked, eyes wide.

"Fuckin' bitch hit me!"

"Look man, I'm all about having fun, but yo' ass is a little out of control," Zach said, looking at Brad and Rob.

"Please, I know yo ass ain't talkin', all the shit I've seen you do!"

"Yeah, but I don't be tryin' to hit no woman," Zach shot back.

"I didn't hit…" Brad stopped himself. He calmed down. "Ya'll trippin'."

"Whatever, man. Let's just get the hell outta here," Rob said. Brad's friends could see that he was ashamed of what he had done. His shoulders slumped, and his head shook.

"I told ya'll I didn't wanna go out."

"Well damn, man, you should have just said so," Zach replied. Brad and Rob gave Zach a look as they walked to the door.

When they returned from the bathroom people stared at them. One woman pointed to Brad and said, "there he is." She shot him an evil glare. The three buddies ignored her and everyone else as they headed for the parking lot. As they drove off. Brad stretched out in the back seat.

"I'm starvin'," Brad said, with a deep sigh.

"Dude, all I want to do is take your ass home," Rob replied.

"C'mon, Rob. I'm cool." Brad looked exhausted. "I just had too much to drink."

"I'm kind of hungry, too," Zach added.

Rob continued to drive, not saying a word.

Noticing the silence, Zach turned and looked at Brad. Brad stared blankly out of the window. "Dude, are you cryin'?"

Brad was so out of it he didn't even hear Zach. "Brad. Are you all right?" Zach asked. Brad looked at him, eyes glazed. Rob looked at Brad in the rearview mirror.

"My life is all fucked up." Brad wiped a tear from the corner of his eye. "Man, I had a good woman and just threw it all away. And for what? Some chick I don't even like. I mean, the sex was cool, but I had a good woman. She was funny, smart, successful, plus I really loved her. And I let her slip away. Fuck,

I'm so hungry." Rob and Zach listened not saying a word. Their boy was opening up like none of them had ever done before. And they felt bad for him, not just because his fiancée left him, but because they dragged him out when they should of listened to him and left him at home.

"There's a Denny's just up ahead," Rob said.

FIFTEEN

Mark drove his Buick through a residential neighborhood in Culver City, and pulled up in front of his house. "I'm gonna run in and get some blankets real quick." He hopped out and sprinted to the front door.

"Bring something to drink," Dolores shouted out of the window. Mark signaled that he heard her.

"So, David, were you born in LA?" Dolores asked.

"Born and raised."

"You're not married, huh?" Dolores asked smiling, clearly a little drunk.

"Oh damn, Dolores," Liz said.

"Did I say something wrong?"

"No. No, I'm not married. I'm divorced," David said with a smile.

"Oh, sorry. So why...?" Dolores asked. Liz interrupted Dolores.

"Dolores, will you shut up? You're bringing me down!"

Mark ran back to the car carrying blankets and a bag. He opened the trunk and put everything inside, then hopped in the car.

"Let's roll," Mark said. He winked at Liz and started up the car and punched it.

By the time they got to the beach, they were all drunk and laughing hysterically. Dolores stopped to watch the waves crashing on the shore and the moonlight hitting the ocean. Mark pulled the blankets out of the trunk.

"Excuse us, boys, I have to talk with my girl for a second," Liz said.

Dolores and Liz trudged across the sand toward the water, holding their shoes in their hands. Dolores stumbled a little bit and Liz grinned.

"What are you smilin' at?" Dolores asked.

"You," Liz said, continuing to grin at Dolores.

"What?" Dolores asked with a smile.

"Hmm, Dolores is about to get some dick," Liz said, taunting her with a gigantic smile.

"Will you shut up!"

"He's cute," Liz said.

"Yeah, he is, isn't he." Dolores looked behind her at the guys coming from the car carrying blankets, and a couple of bags.

"And will you not bring up his ex-wife or Brad? Just enjoy yourself, and don't tell him you're a virgin." Dolores shot Liz a serious look. Then she busted out in laughter. Liz shook her head back and forth. They were like two giddy schoolgirls. Liz went into her purse and pulled out four condoms. "Here. I know you didn't come prepared," Liz said.

"I knew you would be."

"Oh, give me two of those back, I gave you too many." Dolores laughed and handed her two condoms back. Mark and David jogged up from behind.

"Hey ladies, whatcha talkin' 'bout?" Mark asked.

"C'mon," Liz said to Mark. She grabbed Mark by the hand and they headed off toward the water, putting some distance between David and Dolores.

The moon lit up the water and most of the beach just right. The night was warm and breezy, with nothing but the sound of waves crashing on the beach, then sizzling as the water returned from where it came. It was like a sound effect on a sound stage, with the beautiful ocean as a backdrop. They could not have picked a more perfect night.

Liz and Mark were kissing on their blanket fifty yards from Dolores and David. Mark took off Liz's shirt and gently kissed her neck. Liz loved it. Her neck was probably the most sensitive part of her body. However, because of the warm air, she was able to withstand Marks warm tongue and lips.

Dolores and David kissed passionately, tongues intertwined, making their hearts beat fast. Suddenly Dolores stopped and pulled a wine cooler out of a paper bag. She looked at Liz and Mark from a distance.

"I wonder what they're doing?" Dolores asked.

David's eyes were focused more on her.

"Probably what we should be doin'."

"Oh, yeah, and what's that?"

"You know, bumpin' bodies," David said, then laughed. Dolores laughed as well.

"You know I'm a virgin?" Dolores said, out of nowhere. David's smile quickly disappeared and his face grew serious, then he laughed.

"Get the hell outta here."

Dolores laughed with David, then became serious.

"No em', I'm serious." Dolores started to get nervous. However, her eyes still flirted, partly from attraction and partly from the alcohol.

"Oh." David took a moment. "Is something wrong with it?" Dolores gave a little chuckle, thrown off by what he said.

"No, nothing's wrong with it. What's wrong with you men?" She laughed. " I was just saving myself for, you know, marriage, but now I'm just fed up with men and tired of waiting." She took a swig from her wine cooler.

Liz and Mark were in the throes of having sex under a blanket. They were moaning very loud. "Oh, Goddamn! Yes, yes, that's it, right there!" Liz said, in a way that would make any man want to be all he could be.

As the waves crashed on the shore, Mark continued to respond to Liz's seductive voice. Liz smiled, loving the reaction she was getting. She knew she was in control, and that Mark would do whatever she wanted him to do.

David and Dolores were both feeling the tension of having sex. "Well damn, If you've waited this long, I don't wanna mess with that," David said, with sincerity.

"But I want to. And the fact that you just said that makes me want to even more."

"Damn, are you sure?" David asked, conflicted by what he felt in his heart and what he felt in his pants.

"Yeah, I'm sure."

"Well, tell me a little bit about yourself," David said.

"I work for an advertising agency, only child, daughter of Jackie and Lenny King. Now I'm tired of talking," Dolores spit out like rapid fire. She then stared at him like he was the answer to all of her lonely nights—and most of all her horny ones. David lay back, staring up at her, eyes wide. Dolores smiled then threw her wine cooler behind her.

"You're not gonna hurt me are you?" David asked, joking.

"No, I'm not gonna hurt you," Dolores said sexually, but very serious. They stared into each other's eyes, hearts pounding faster and faster. Dolores slipped off her blouse, showing her perfect C cup breasts. David smiled. She gave him a soft kiss, with only a little tongue. She then helped him a little, as he eased off her pants and panties. They kissed passionately, and Dolores stuck her hand down David's pants and gave him a squeeze. She smiled at him, impressed. Dolores unbuckled his belt and unbuttoned his pants. She slid his pants down. She pulled the blanket over them, covering most of their bodies. She reached over into her purse and pulled out a condom and handed it to him. Their eyes remained locked on each other. David slipped the condom on under the blanket. They kissed again. David maneuvered on top of her, kissing her neck and then her breast. He sucked her nipples, making them hard and erect. Dolores closed her eyes and let out a deep sigh.

Liz was on top of Mark like she was riding a horse. "Oh, that feels so good, you better not come. Oh God, you better not come. Don't you come. Oh, don't, you, come." On the downstroke Liz noticed a beach patrol truck pulling up on Dolores and David.

"Oh shit!" Liz said.

David was on top of Dolores, kissing her passionately. He scooted up and prepared to thrust himself into her. Suddenly, a spotlight hit both of them.

"Shit!"

Dolores covered her face with the blanket. "Oh damn, I'm so embarrassed," she said to herself. Dolores and David sat up with the blanket still covering most of them, shamed. A patrol officer spoke over the intercom.

"The beach is closed. You folks have to exit the beach," the patrol officer said.

"We're leaving right now," Dolores shouted. The two officers in the truck chuckled, staring, hoping to sneak a peak. David threw his hands up in the air as if to say, is there anything else?

"Thank you very much," the officer responded. Both of the officers laughed over the intercom while driving off.

Liz and David fell asleep on the drive back. Dolores looked deep in thought, staring out of her window, then at David. Mark pulled up in front of the club where Liz left her car. "All right, we're here," he said. David woke up, looking around. Liz slowly opened her eyes. Half asleep, she smiled and kissed Mark.

"All right, Mark, give me a call, okay?"

"Oh, without a doubt. We got some unfinished business to take care of."

"Hmm, you got that right," Liz responded with a quickness.

"So you're gonna call me?" Dolores asked.

David hesitated. "Yeah, I'll give you a call sometime this week all right." His eyes were shifty. It was clear that he was not telling the truth. Dolores smiled and gave him a kiss on the cheek. She knew.

"What?" David asked.

"Nothing," Dolores said. The ladies got out of the car.

Dolores and Liz drove home dog-tired.

"Damn! Why'd you take so long?" Liz asked, frustrated and amused by the whole thing.

"I didn't know it was a race," Dolores replied.

"So how close did you get?"

"His dick was damn near sittin' on it." Dolores laughed, then Liz joined her. "I think I'm cursed," Dolores said, as she continued to crack up.

 # SIXTEEN

Tony stormed into Dolores' office, eyes scattered, voice higher than normal. "Dolores, tell me you've moved the accounting files for the "Lays account!"

Dolores sighed, leaned back in her chair, and crossed her legs.

"No, I haven't messed with the files," Dolores said. Tony paused for a second, then rushed out of the office. A smile crept across Dolores' face.

Bently sat at his desk, glaring at Tony. Tony looked like a kid being reprimanded by his teacher. "What do you mean you can't find the files?" Bently asked. "Is everyone losin' it around here?"

"I looked on my computer, and they weren't there."

"Well look again."

"I've looked three times already."

"I said look again!"

There was a knock on the door. Bently looked at Tony with disgust. "Come in!"

Dolores stepped in. Bently had a huge crease in the center of his forehead. His mind was in 'fix it' mode. "Dolores, can you come back in five minutes?" His eyes remained on Tony, and his mind on the problem at hand.

"I found the files," Dolores said. Bently and Tony looked at her, surprised. "Yeah, they were on the server; you must of just overlooked them."

Tony stood frozen. Bently let out a huge sigh.

"Thank you, Dolores." Bently looked at Tony, shaking his head.

Tony smiled at Dolores as if to say, 'you got me.' Dolores smiled back as if to say, 'I know.'

◻◻◻◻

Dolores and Liz laughed hysterically over lunch in the cafeteria. "That shit is so funny to me," Liz said.

"You should have seen the look on his face," Dolores gloated.

"That's what men get for underestimating women."

Dolores and Liz gave each other a high-five. Then Dolores stopped.

"Oh my God, I think I feel bad."

"Please! He deserved it."

"I don't know, I just keep feeling like it wasn't totally his fault. You should have heard the way his wife was talkin' to him." Liz looked unsympathetic. "I mean, you've seen her; she looks so damn innocent, but she's really a monster."

"I'm sure she's not that bad," Liz said, amused.

"Total bitch. She was actually forcing him and he was telling her, enough's enough."

"Well, that's what he gets for being influenced so damn easily." Liz looked up and saw Tony heading to their table. "Hmm, look who's comin'," Liz said. Dolores turned around.

"Hey, can I talk to you for a minute?" Tony asked Dolores politely.

"Sure…"

"You can have my seat. I gotta go make some phone calls." Liz grabbed her purse and walked off. Tony sat down. Dolores and Tony looked at each other, waiting for someone to begin the conversation. The tension grew. "Look!" Tony and Dolores said at the same time. They both gave a smirk.

"You first," Dolores said.

"Why don't we try to start over?" Tony asked.

"I think that's a good idea," Dolores replied in a calm voice.

"Hmm."

"Hmm."

"Great," Tony said.

Dolores sighed. "You know, you started it."

Tony returned her sigh.

"I know," Tony said, calm and cool. Dolores was surprised—and impressed that he admitted it. "Look, Bently said that we have to work on this Lays account together. He seems to think that we would work better together." Dolores thought about it for a moment.

"Okay," Dolores said.

Tony extended his hand and Dolores shook it. They watched each other closely, looking for any signs of insincerity.

 **SEVENTEEN**

Dolores was in the grocery store on a mission: get a half-gallon of pecan praline ice cream and a pack of chocolate chip cookies. She loved this little merger of ice cream and cookies, but she only risked losing her figure to this deadly combination when she was extremely stressed.

She walked up and down the aisles looking for other things that could go against her five-day-a-week workout routine. She picked up a bag of Hershey Kisses, then thought about the damage they would do. She threw them back in the rack. She got her ice cream and cookies and headed to the register.

As she waited in line, she glanced at a picture of Oprah on the cover of a magazine. She thought about how beautiful she was and, most of all, how necessary to the world she had become. She wondered if she would ever become that successful and important.

"Excuse me; don't I know you?" a deep voice asked from behind. Dolores rolled her eyes, not in the mood to be hit on or bothered. She turned around and saw that it was Trey, the tall, dark, handsome brotha from the nightclub. She was caught off guard, and was uncomfortable in his presence. He smiled, showing off perfectly aligned white teeth. His smile was beautiful. Dolores didn't notice how nice his smile was in the club, but now she was almost amazed by it.

"Liz's friend, right?" he asked.

"Uh, yeah."

"Hi, I'm Trey."

"Hi." Dolores acted like she didn't remember him.

"You remember me, right?" Trey asked.

"Uh, no." Dolores patted her hair, feeling self-conscious because it wasn't done.

"You were checking me out at the club," Trey said, flashing his killer smile.

"I was not checking you out, you were checking me out."

"Ah, so you do remember me."

Dolores smiled, knowing she was caught. "Yeah, weren't you the bartender?"

"You remember me. I wasn't no damn bartender."

They both laughed.

Dolores paid for her ice cream and cookies and Trey walked her to her car. Their attraction to one another was evident. They talked in the parking lot for over an hour, then Trey asked Dolores if she wanted to come over his house so he could show her his DVD collection. They both knew that wasn't all he wanted to show her.

Dolores followed Trey's car through the city. "Girl, just go home. What are you doing?" Dolores said to herself. "What are you doing? He could be a murderer. Hell, you don't know this man," Dolores said, looking at her reflection in the rearview mirror. She stopped at a red light, but Trey continued through the intersection. Dolores hoped he would keep going, not realizing she was no longer behind him. She was hoping that by him losing her he would be making the decision for her. "That's right, keep goin', so I can go home, eat my ice cream, masturbate and go to sleep." Suddenly, the brake lights on Trey's Mustang lit up. "Shit." The light turned green and she continued to follow him. "What am I doing?" she asked herself again as she pulled up in front of his home in Baldwin Hills. It was a small house, but hey, she was just impressed that a brotha had a house in the hills. The garage door opened and Trey pulled inside. Dolores parked on the street and sat in the car, contemplating whether to drive off or not. Suddenly, Trey knocked on her window. She jumped.

"You getting out?" He waved her in. Dolores got out.

"I'm gonna have to put my ice cream in your freezer."

"Whatever, girl. C'mon, you can eat it here if you want."

Trey's house had a sprawling view of the city. Dolores loved the view. His house was probably the size of a small apartment, but the view made it look extremely fly. Trey apologized for the mess as he picked up a couple pair of shorts and shirts. And a pair of red panties. He didn't say anything about them and neither did Dolores. Trey knew what kind of guy he was, and wasn't ashamed of it. He quickly showed her his DVD collection, then gave her a tour of the rest of the house.

As the night went on they drank a little wine. They laughed and joked. It almost seemed weird to Dolores to feel so comfortable with a complete stranger. But Trey was so charming and sexy, she really didn't care.

"So now that you got me here, what are you going to do with me?" Dolores asked.

"I don't know. Maybe just let you give me a back massage so I can go to sleep," Trey said, smiling.

"Really."

"Really."

Eventually Dolores found herself sitting on Trey's bed with nothing but a towel wrapped around her. Her brown skin shone from the shower she took and the baby oil she put on.

Trey stood over her with a cocky grin. "Girl, I'm not gonna front. I'm nothin' to play with," he said. He wore nothing but a towel around his waist, while beads of water trickled down his body. Dolores looked at him, not saying a word. She was turned on by him staring down at her like she was his prey. Her chest rose and fell faster and faster. She swallowed, searching for the moisture in her mouth that was no longer there. "I'm gonna fuck the shit out of you, bitch."

Dolores was caught off guard.

"Excuse me?"

"You heard me. I'm gonna tear that ass up."

"Trey, don't talk like that."

"Talk like what?"

"Dirty."

"Oh, my bad; some women like that." Trey leaned over and kissed her on the lips soft and gentle. She stood up.

"That's better," Dolores said, kissing him back. She could see her problem solver rising under his towel. She smiled, realizing he was the perfect man for the job.

"Who's your daddy?" Trey asked, as he tugged her hair.

"Huh?"

"You heard me. Now who's your daddy?" He tugged her hair again.

"You are, I guess," Dolores answered, unsure. She looked at him strangely.

"That's right! I'm about to tear this shit up." He gripped her ass tightly.

"Shit. Tear up?" She pulled back. "I don't want you to tear up anything."

"C'mon baby, let me beat up this ass like you know you want me to."

"Wow." Dolores said, staring up at him blankly.

As Dolores drove off, Trey stood on his porch with the towel wrapped around his waist covering his erect penis. "That's some ole bullshit," he muttered as he strolled back into his house.

 **EIGHTEEN**

Dolores stared in the mirror as she put on her makeup. Her hair was done and she looked beautiful. She noticed that she looked sad. She smiled, hoping to get the sadness out of her eyes. But even with an exaggerated smile, she could not make the sadness disappear.

 口 口 口 口

Liz lounged in her living room on the couch, drinking with Damon, an attractive thirty-two-year-old man. His little brother Bobby was also there; Bobby was twenty-one and muscular, and very sexy. The doorbell rang. "Oh, that's my girl right there," Liz said as she hopped up. She opened the door to Dolores wearing a smirk on her face. "Hey you guys, this is my friend Dolores."

"Hello," Dolores said, smiling.

"Hey, Dolores. I've met you over here before. Damon," he said, trying to jog her memory.

Dolores looked back at him bewildered. "Oh yeah," she said, not knowing who the hell he was. She thought to herself that Liz had so many men over there, he could have killed someone right in front of her, and she still wouldn't have remembered him. Dolores looked at Bobby sitting on the sofa.

"Hi. My name's Bobby."

Dolores did a double take, realizing that although he was handsome, he was also very young.

"Hi. How are you doin'?" Dolores said to Bobby, with a lazy wave.

"You want something to drink, girl?" Liz asked.

"Uh yeah, just get me some wine. Wait a minute, I'll go with you." Dolores followed Liz into the kitchen. Liz got the wine out of the refrigerator. "How old is that boy in there?" Dolores asked. Liz gave a little laugh.

"Why?"

"Because I wanna know."

"You always have to be so damn difficult."

"How old?" Dolores asked, in a stern tone.

"Twenty-one."

"Damn girl! I'm old enough to be his... teenaged mama!"

"Will you calm down," Liz said, letting out a laugh. Liz handed Dolores a drink. "Look, he's Damon's little brother."

"He's his brother? They don't even look alike."

"They got different mamas. Look, if you don't like him, don't talk to him."

"Hmm."

"Don't try to act like you haven't noticed the fact that the boy is fine and got a slammin' body."

"Looks aren't everything, Liz."

"But it's something. Something good."

"What does he do?"

"He goes to college in Florida. He plays football."

"Hmm."

"C'mon, girl."

Liz and Dolores entered the living room carrying a bottle of wine and a couple of glasses. "Let's play cards," Liz said.

"I don't wanna play no cards," Dolores replied.

"You have some dominos?" Damon asked.

"Nope," Liz responded.

"I got an idea. Let's play 'Truth Or Dare'," Bobby said as he sipped his drink. Dolores, Liz, and Damon looked at each other as if Bobby had said something wrong. Everyone except Bobby busted out in laughter. "What? What I say?"

"You have to excuse my little bro'; he's a bit young," Damon said, still laughing. The ladies continued to laugh. Bobby gave a sarcastic laugh as well.

"Forget y'all," Bobby said, smiling.

"Damn, that was like a straight flashback to college," Liz said, still laughing.

"Who you tellin'," Dolores added. Liz gave Dolores a funny look.

"You always was the little scaredy cat that wouldn't play," Liz said to Dolores, as she took a sip of her wine.

"No I wasn't."

"Always makin' excuses why not to play," Liz added, taking another sip with a mischievous grin.

"All I know is that you guys looked at me like I stole somethin'," Bobby said. "Shit, it's just a game."

"No, it's not that. Just when you've been out of school for ten years, it kind of comes off as well, young," Dolores said, as though she was schooling Bobby on the art of adulthood. Liz shot Dolores a sarcastic look.

"Fuck it. I say we play!" Liz spit out.

"Play what?!" Dolores shot back.

"I'm down. Good idea bro'," Damon said.

"Cool; let's play," Bobby said, sitting up.

"I'm not playing no "Truth or Dare," Dolores said, rolling her eyes.

"Why not?" Liz asked.

"Cause I said so."

"Well, that's cool. We don't have to play. It was just an idea," Bobby said.

"Sound like a fun idea to me," Damon said, with a big smile plastered across his face.

"Me too, Dolores!" Liz said, giving her an evil glare.

"I thought I escaped this stupid-ass game in college. All right, c'mon," Dolores said. Everyone laughed and cheered Dolores on. "All right. Just don't nobody ask any degrading questions!" Dolores said, shaking her head as if she could not believe what she just agreed to.

"It ain't even like that," Bobby said.

Liz frowned and crossed her arms like a thug off the street. "Dolores, you startin' to act like a real bitch right now. You actin' like a little ho. I don't care what these fools ask, we gonna handle it like G's, okay?" Liz said intensely, trying her best to sound like a killer. Everyone laughed hysterically.

"You are so stupid. And you watch too many damn gangster movies," Dolores said, rolling her eyes.

"All right, y'all ready?" Bobby asked.

"Yeah, yeah , c'mon," Dolores replied.

"Who's gonna start?" Damon asked.

"Why don't you start, since you're the little genius that thought of the game," Dolores said to Bobby.

"Hey, I just play it; I didn't invent it. But it would be my pleasure to start the game with you beautiful women. Liz," Bobby said, peering at her intensely.

"Whatcha want?" Liz said nonchalantly. Everyone laughed, sipping their drinks and becoming more tipsy.

"Truth or Dare?" Bobby shot at her like a prosecutor in a courtroom.

"Truth."

"Are you guys just gonna keep saying truth all night?" Bobby asked.

"No, this is just foreplay. Now go," Liz said.

"All right, but first I must warn you I am very experienced in this game. I've made people cry, lie, fight, and you know what." Bobby insinuated sex with his eyes. He was intense, and very serious. Everyone chuckled, sipping their drinks, admiring the young man's spunk.

"Yeah, yeah, me too," Liz said.

"Okay. Have you ever sucked a dick!?" Bobby asked aggressively, almost yelling.

"Why, yes I have. Big black ones. My turn," Liz answered without a care in the world. Everyone laughed. Bobby's eyebrows shot up, impressed with Liz's response.

"Your technique is good," Bobby stated, eyes wide, shaking his head slowly, wearing a smirk on his face.

"I know. Okay, Bobby, "Truth or Dare?" Liz asked in a calm, sensuous tone.

"Dare." Bobby sat back folding his arms, accepting the challenge.

"I dare you to kiss Dolores passionately for…"

"What?!" Dolores shouted.

"Shut up, Dolores. Sixty seconds. And kiss her like she's your woman that you haven't seen in ten years," Liz said, eager to see this happen. Everyone got extremely giddy. "All right, go 'head," Liz said, shooting Dolores a funny look.

"C'mon Bobby," Dolores said, just wanting to get it over with. Bobby got up and leaned toward Dolores, looking very sexy. She could see his rock-hard biceps under his short-sleeved shirt as he reached toward her. "Got me robbin' the cradle kissing this young boy," Dolores said under her breath.

"I ain't that young," Bobby replied, with a sexy smile, looking beyond his years. Dolores liked his lips. She watched him give them a quick lick, as he moved in closer. He kissed her softly and passionately at first, then hard and long like a real pro. Dolores started to enjoy it. A lot. Damon smiled, looking at Liz.

"Keep goin'," Liz said, wearing a huge smile while taking a sip of her drink. Liz got up and grabbed Damon by his hand, dimmed the lights, and quietly strolled to the bedroom. Dolores and Bobby continued to kiss. They finally stopped and looked around, and saw that they were all alone. They laughed, a little embarrassed.

"I guess Liz is getting her fix," Dolores said.

"I guess so."

"So, Bobby, you play football, huh?"

"Yep."

"Yeah, you got one of those football heads." They both laughed.

"Is that right?"

"Yeah, you know you guys be havin' those muscle heads that are flat on top, with a few dents on the side."

Bobby laughed.

Dolores thought he was sexy—and his bulging biceps didn't hurt his looks either.

"My goodness: What have I done to receive this type of abuse?"

"Here; come here," Dolores said. She sat on the couch and gestured for him to sit on the floor between her legs. He scooted to her. She felt around his head examining it.

"I know what you're thinking," Bobby said, liking her fingers playing in his scalp.

"Oh yeah? And what's that?"

"This man has a pretty sexy head, and no dents," Bobby said, as his eyes rolled back in his head.

"Yeah, you got a nice head, but what does that mean? You ride the bench?" Dolores chuckled and Bobby looked at her.

"Whatever," Bobby shot back, then smiled, amused.

"Don't get all mad."

"Girl, you don't faze me."

Dolores looked at Bobby as if she was being turned on by him. "Hmm, too bad you're so young." Dolores shook her head as if she had to pass up her favorite dessert.

"Too bad you're so old."

Dolores' jaw dropped. "I am not old!"

"Well, I'm not so young!"

"All right, touché!"

"That's right," Bobby said, with a sly smile.

Dolores ran her hand along the side of his neck. Bobby turned and kissed Dolores. She rubbed his broad, muscular shoulders. She thought about his age and how he was too young for her, but the more they kissed, the more she realized that he was definitely a man. A young man, but a man nevertheless.

They were kissing passionately, and could hear the "oohs" and "ahs" of love making coming from Liz's bedroom. As the moans got louder, the headboard started knocking. Dolores and Bobby stopped kissing. They looked at the wall, then at each other, and laughed. Then Dolores suddenly got serious. "You have a condom?"

"Huh?" Bobby was totally caught off guard. He swallowed the lump in his throat, but before he could answer Dolores repeated herself.

"Do you have a condom?"

"Nah, but shit I'm cool. I ain't got nothin'," Bobby said earnestly.

"Go get a condom," Dolores instructed Bobby with a smile, almost as if he was a student and she was his teacher.

"Well I didn't drive, Damon did."

"Well, where's his keys?"

"He got em'." They could still hear the headboard pounding against the wall.

"Well just forget it."

"I saw a store about two miles back. I can just run over there," Bobby said like an addict needing a fix. He jumped up and headed toward the door.

"Bobby, just forget it."

"It ain't no problem. I needed to get my workout on anyway," Bobby shot back as he dashed out. Dolores sat on the couch listening to Damon and Liz having sex.

"Oh yes, yes, hell yes, oh goddamn," Liz yelled.

"Oh shit, ohh shit!" Damon shouted as if he was in pain. A good pain.

Dolores shook her head, amused. Then a seriousness came over her as she thought about when she was a kid.

旦旦旦旦

A twelve-year-old Dolores walked with her mother through the local supermarket. Jackie held her hand, pulling her along. Dolores was on the verge of crying, holding her stomach as if she had a bellyache. They walked straight to the shelf full of tampons. Dolores took one look at them, and burst into tears. Jackie comforted her. "Baby, baby, no, it's not that bad. This is something that every woman goes through."

"Can't I just make it go away for at least two more years?" Dolores asked, sobbing.

Jackie gave a light chuckle. "Baby, you can't control these kinds of things."

"It's a girl at our school who stopped hers by getting surgery. Can't I just do that?"

"Trust me, she did not get surgery. This is just part of becoming a woman."

"So what does this mean, that your body's ready for sex or something?"

"No! Look, sex has to be special, like with your husband. You don't just do it to do it. You do it because it means something. Otherwise it's a big waste of time, your time and his." She let out a huge sigh, then looked at her little girl as if she was going to tell her the most important thing in the world. "Just remember, when you get older and fall in love and get married and have sex, in that order, you're falling for a man because of his heart, and not because of what's going on between your legs. You got that?"

"Yes."

"Because a man will treat you the way you allow him to treat you." Dolores gazed up into her mother's eyes, realizing what her mother was saying was to be taken to heart. Dolores wiped her tears. They held each other tight. "And when you get married and make love with your husband for the first time, you'll be glad you waited. And when you have kids, and you don't want any more, you gonna be happy to see that period come every month." Dolores quickly pulled back from Jackie, startled.

"What do you mean every month!?" Dolores shouted.

꒝ ꒝ ꒝ ꒝

Dolores sat on Liz's sofa thinking. She never forgot that discussion with her mother. Her mom always talked to her straight—as if she was an adult. And that's why the two of them could talk about anything when Dolores was growing up. But as she got older, Dolores felt her mother was a little too much involved and seemed to want to know everything that went on in her life. This is why she felt she had to spread her wings and go to college out of state.

Dolores continued to wait for Bobby. "What am I doin'?" Dolores asked herself as she waited for Bobby's penis with a condom on it. "I'm better than this."

When Bobby opened the door, Dolores stood there with her coat on looking apologetic. "What's wrong?" he asked.

"Nothing. It's just time for me to go home, I'm sorry."

"But why?" Bobby's face fell and his shoulders slumped.

"Hey, this isn't my style. I'm not gonna sleep with a man I hardly know," Dolores said, feeling good about her decision.

"Are you sure? I got the condoms," Bobby said, holding up the package he just bought.

Dolores thought he was cute, looking at her like a one-of-a-kind piece of artwork that he couldn't possess. She smiled at him.

"Positive. Look, I'm sorry. I feel so bad I got you out there runnin' the streets like a mad man looking for condoms." They laughed. Bobby tried to mask his disappointment, but his eyes showed he still wanted her. "I'm just not like that, I'm sorry." Bobby looked her up and down almost in pain.

"Don't worry about it. I'll be all right. I think." He gave a little laugh. "So can I get your number at least?" Bobby asked.

"Sure."

They both knew at that moment that this would probably be the last time they would see each other. But just like she did with the brotha from the beach, she gave him her number anyway.

NINETEEN

Dolores and Tony rushed around her office handling the business of the day. Working with Tony had turned out to be better than she anticipated. Bently saw that they worked well together, so he gave them the Lays account to complete—the company's biggest account in ten years. They knew they had to bring their "A" game.

⊔⊓⊔⊓

Tony rushed inside his house taking off his clothes as he looked for Mary. "Mary!"

He looked in the kitchen then the family room.

"Mary, where you at!"

There was still no answer. Tony marched into his bedroom. At first there was no sign of Mary, but then he took a closer look at the bed covered with blankets.

"Mary, wake up!" He could see a foot exposed from under the covers. "Mary."

"What?"

Mary started to unravel herself from the covers. "I'm not goin'," she said with a frog in her throat, barely opening her eyes.

"What are you talking about?" Tony pulled back some of the covers.

"I don't wanna go." Mary pulled the covers back.

"I told you this is important!"

"Tony, you don't need me. Shit, you might as well take Dolores. You been spending more time with her anyway."

"What?"

"You heard what I said."

"She's my co-worker."

"Are you sure? Cause you sure have been skippin' around here lovin' goin' to work lately."

"So I'm supposed to not like my job now?"

"Whatever, man."

"Look, put a dress on and get ready."

"No."

"Don't play with me. Get dressed!"

"I said no!!" Mary shot back with a menacing stare.

Tony took a deep breath, and exhaled. He walked into the bathroom and turned on the shower. He leaned over the bathroom sink, staring into the basin, then at his reflection in the mirror. He started to laugh—too through with Mary's behavior.

Mary lay in bed, fuming. But when she heard Tony laughing in the bathroom, her anger slowly disappeared. She got out of bed and strolled to her closet, which was filled with beautiful dresses and tons of shoes. She picked up a pair of tan shoes. Then grabbed a dress to match.

"Damn, I don't wanna go to this thing," she said to herself.

回 卩回 卩

Limousines packed the Hilton Hotel driveway. The ballroom was rocking to a live band. Liz and Dolores strolled in, looking beautiful and socializing as they worked the room.

Dolores was surrounded by her co-workers. "Everybody looks so nice. Where's the old man at?" Dolores asked.

"Oh, Bently's over there talking to Robert."

"I see him," Dolores replied.

"I heard you and Tony nailed that Lays account," the man to her left said.

"Yes we did," Dolores said with relief.

"Hello, Dolores," the man across from her said in passing.

"Hello," Dolores responded.

"Congratulations on that account," an older gentleman said.

"Oh, thank you." Dolores smiled.

"Save me a dance, all right?" the older man said.

"Okay." Dolores rolled her eyes, smiling.

"Yeah, I heard you and Tony are like the dynamic duo," another man said.

"Is that right?" Dolores asked, loving all the attention.

"Yeah, Bently keeps saying how well you guys work together."

"I have to give it to him—Tony's a hard worker," Dolores added. She wore a smile. She now admired Tony as a co-worker and a friend. She knew they had come a long way.

"There he is, right there." The man pointed to Tony walking toward them. Dolores' smile quickly disappeared when she saw Mary on his arm.

"Congratulations, partner!" Tony said, reaching out for a hug. The two gave a quick embrace.

"Thank you; you too," Dolores replied. Mary was smiling, but her eyes said what was really on her mind. She wanted to squash Dolores like a bug.

"Hello, Dolores," Mary said with a smile that could bite.

"Hello, how you doin'?" Dolores replied, returning the same fake smile. Dolores looked around.

"Where did Liz go?" Dolores asked.

"I think she went to the bar," a woman said.

Out of nowhere Liz approached with a drink in her hand.

"You guys should go get a drink," Liz said.

"Liz don't waste no time," Dolores said, shaking her head. As everyone headed to the bar, Liz pulled Dolores aside.

"Look at this bitch acting like a few weeks ago she wasn't tryin' to get yo' ass fired," Liz said, staring at Mary.

"I am in too good of a mood to be thinking about her ass. Come on, I need to get my drink on," Dolores responded. They headed toward the bar wearing matching smiles.

As the night went on, Dolores, Liz, Tony, Mary and a few of their co-workers sat at a table drinking. They all looked a little tipsy, laughing louder than normal.

"So, Dolores, are you gonna take a vacation soon?" Mary asked.

"No, I don't have time for anything but work right now."

"Isn't that the truth," Tony cosigned.

"Is that right?" Mary said to Tony.

"You know what I'm talkin' about," Tony said, not trying to go there.

"No, Tony, what are you talking about?"

"So Mary, I heard that you guys got a new house." Dolores interrupted, trying to change the subject.

"Oh yeah, it's okay," Mary said, not appreciating the subject change. Tony looked at Mary.

"Just okay," Tony responded, a little ticked.

"I mean it's not the best house I've ever seen," Mary said.

"But it's ours. And it's in expensive-ass LA," Tony added, shaking his head with disbelief. Liz and Dolores looked at each other. Tony let out a huge sigh, trying his best to contain himself. "C'mon, I don't wanna argue tonight." Tony attempted to cut the tension between them.

"Whatever." Mary waved him off. Tony bit his bottom lip slightly embarrassed. He tried to play it off by smiling. Then he stood and reached his hand out.

"C'mon sweetheart, let's dance," Tony said.

"No!" Mary said with a look that would kill.

Liz burst out in laughter and Dolores nudged her with an elbow. Liz stopped laughing immediately, trying her best to contain herself.

"C'mon, don't be like that." Tony smiled, trying to play it off. He stood there with his hand out for what seemed like an eternity. Everyone sat stunned, watching them go back and forth like they were watching a tennis match.

"I said no! I don't feel like it. Ask someone else." Tony sat back down. Liz continued to try to contain her laughter. "Ask your partner," Mary said, giving a sharp nod to Dolores.

"Sure, I'd love to," Dolores said. She got up and grabbed Tony by the hand. They strolled to the dance floor. Tony did not look back at Mary and neither did Dolores. Her response surprised Mary, and made her more irritated. Liz sat with her mouth wide open, then she started to snicker. Mary cut her eyes at Liz.

Dolores and Tony slow danced, sharing a smile and a sense of amusement. They were careful not to dance too close, sensing Mary's eyes on them. "She's not as much of a bitch as she seems."

"I'm sure she's not," Dolores said, without any sarcasm in her voice.

"Well, maybe she is." They tried not to laugh.

"Hey, let's just enjoy the fact that the Lays account is done," Dolores said.

"Who you tellin'." They continued to smile.

"So are you going to miss Tom?" Dolores asked.

"Yeah, I just can't believe he's retired, but I'm happy for him."

"He's a good man."

"Dolores, uh, I just want you to know that I won't have no hard feelings if you get Tom's job. You deserve it," he said with sincerity.

"Is that right?"

"After all, you have been here longer," Tony said.

"Well, thank you," Dolores said in a playful, sarcastic tone. "And if you get it, I won't have any hard feelings either." They let it soak in while continuing to dance like brother and sister, respecting the woman who was sitting at the table staring at them with an evil glare.

TWENTY

Bently sat at his desk, Dolores and Tony seated across from him. "I want you to know that this was an extremely hard decision to make, but it had to be made." Bently took a moment; he knew that the disappointment of one of his best employees was inevitable. "I've decided to give the position to Tony." Tony and Dolores stared blankly, trying their best not to show any emotion. "Now, Dolores, this is no reflection on you; it's just that Tony has the most experience overall."

"I think I need to say something," Tony said.

Dolores put her hand on his leg, stopping him. "Tony, I just want to say, I'm very happy for you. You deserve it," Dolores said with a smile. Tony's face was ridden with guilt.

"Congratulations," Bently said to Tony.

"Thank you, sir."

Tony strolled into his beautiful home. It was a three-bedroom house with a large kitchen, a family room, and a pool. He entered the living room, face drawn. Mary joined him. She looked beautifully pampered in her lavender silk robe and manicured feet. "Hey, babe, how's it going?" she asked.

"Fine."

"You hungry?"

"No, I'm fine."

"What's the matter?" Mary asked. She spoke in a soft, loving voice.

"Nothing," Tony said, letting all the air out of his chest.

"Sit down for a second." Mary grabbed Tony by the hand and led him to the couch. "Look, I'm sorry I was such a bitch at the party."

"Why are you telling me this?"

"Because I really am sorry. I was being a bitch."

Tony was not impressed with her apology, having heard it too many times to count. Mary kissed Tony on the neck, then the lips. Tony broke into a slight smile. "There's that smile." They both gave a little laugh. Tony kissed her back, not being able to resist her smile or her beautiful eyes.

"Guess what?" Tony said, with an even bigger smile.

"What?"

"I got Tom's job."

"Yes!" Mary screamed. She jumped off the couch and gave him a hug. "Oh my God! How much money will you be making?"

"I'm not sure exactly, I know it's a little over three hundred and fifty thousand, plus bonuses."

"Oh my God!" Mary screamed again. Tony smiled at Mary's reaction. Mary calmed down. "Wow." Her mind was running a hundred miles an hour. She got excited again. "Oh my God, we can get some more new furniture. Oh, I gotta go call Linda so we can go shopping!"

Tony's smile slowly disappeared as he watched Mary run into the bedroom.

"Tony, we can afford that trip to Hawaii first class now!" Mary shouted from the bedroom.

"Yeah, I guess."

"This is so perfect. You're still getting your vacation this week right?"

"Well, if I want it."

"Great, let's go this weekend then," Mary shouted from the bedroom. Tony's face showed his irritation.

"Girl, what you doin' tomorrow? My man got a raise and I'm ready to shop!" Tony heard Mary screaming with laughter.

凹回凹回

Dolores talked on the phone while she shuffled through papers; Liz was at her desk downstairs. "Liz, when you get a chance, send up those numbers for the new account," Dolores said.

"All right. Also, you got some mail down here. I'll send that up too."

"All right."

"Hey girl, I'm going out wit' Mark tonight. What's up with David?" Liz asked.

"Nothing."

"He was cute."

"Being cute isn't enough," Dolores said, looking out the window.

"Well, I'm 'bout to leave, so if you change your mind call me tonight."

"Bye, Liz." As Dolores hung up the phone, someone knocked on the door. "Come in." Tony entered.

"How's it going?" Tony asked, still feeling a little leftover guilt.

"Just busy, that's all."

"Well." Tony's eyes shifted back and forth, as if he had something to say.

"Are you okay?" Dolores asked, sensing the guilt he was still struggling with.

"Yeah, I'm okay."

"You got something on your mind?" Dolores asked. Tony thought about it for a moment.

"Look, I've been thinking about what I did. I don't know, it's…"

"Tony, just forget about it," Dolores interrupted.

"I can't help but think, if I wouldn't have taken those documents that you put in Robert's box, you probably would've gotten Tom's job." Dolores thought about what Tony said for a moment. Then she smiled.

"Are you apologizing?"

"Well, yes," Tony said.

"Well I accept. Plus I went on the server and moved your files. So we're even, all right?"

"Well, I felt like I needed to say something," he said with sincerity, then turned around and headed to the door. He stopped and looked back.

"I'm not sweatin' it, I'll get the next one," Dolores said, reassuring him. Tony paused, taking it all in.

"Dolores, you wanna get a drink after work?"

"Huh?"

"You heard me. I need a drink, and you could probably use one too."

"Uh, no, I can't. I gotta go home and get some sleep."

"All right. I'll see you tomorrow, then." Tony walked out of her office.

ᗡᗡᗡᗡ

Dolores entered her home, burned out. When she reached the kitchen, she opened the refrigerator and grabbed a pint of ice cream. Then she went to her bedroom and took off her clothes. She stretched out on her bed, wearing only her bra and panties. She grabbed the book on the nightstand and started to read. The cover read "Waiting For Mr. Right". The book was recommended to her by Liz, who said that it would make her realize that all men are dogs. It had all kinds of rules that a woman must use to tame her man, and make him be obedient in order for him to be at least a good dog. She didn't take the book too serious—it was silly, but it made her laugh. It also made her think about her life, and what was to come.

Dolores put down the book and rubbed her temples. Her job had consumed her, and she knew it. She also thought about Brad, who was still calling her at least twice a week. Then she wondered whether she made the right decision, not giving him another chance.

ᗡᗡᗡᗡ

Tony sat in the living room. He rotated two silver balls in his hand, lost in thought. He still felt guilty about what he had done to Dolores, and how he accepted a job that might have gone to her if he had not messed with her work. Plus, he had started to really like Dolores, and respect her as a businesswoman and a person. He put on some John Coltrane, stretched out on the couch, and went to sleep. That night he dreamt that Mary took all of his money and left him for a rapper with diamonds on all his teeth. He woke up in a cold sweat.

 # TWENTY-ONE

Dolores and Tony were in their offices working late into the night. Tony typed at his computer while jazz played in the background. Dolores got up from her desk, put on her jacket, and grabbed her briefcase. She walked down the corridor and passed Tony's office twirling her keys. She stopped for a second, hearing jazz playing. She looked at her watch. It was 9:30PM.

Tony stopped typing when he heard a knock on the door. He hesitated for a moment. "Come in."

Dolores opened up the door and peeked in. "I didn't know you were still here," she said, surprised. She noticed he was beaming. "What are you doing?"

Tony hesitated, looking embarrassed. "I'm trying to work on this manuscript I've been putting off for, like, forever."

"Are you serious?" Dolores walked behind Tony's desk and peered at his computer. "What is it about?"

"It's a romantic comedy."

"I didn't know you write."

"Well, I really don't. Only when I get the time. And that's hardly ever."

Dolores looked at the computer screen, then at Tony, impressed.

"I took a creative writing class when I was in college, so it kinda became my little hobby," Tony said.

"I wrote a short story when I was in college, but never wrote again."

"Why'd you stop?" Tony asked, sitting back in his chair.

"I don't have the patience for it. I think I have more of a business mind," Dolores said.

"I used to love to write," Tony said, staring at his monitor.

"Well you should make time; you never know."

"Mary bitches about it a lot." Tony mimicked Mary: "Until you're able to make a livin' doin' it, you need to concentrate on your job. Your real job." They laughed.

"You need to do what makes you happy. If you like to write, write. Hey, you should let me read your work one day."

"All right." They smiled. For a moment they just stared at each other.

"Well, I'm about to go home," Dolores said.

"All right, I'll see you tomorrow."

"Bye," she said as she walked to the door.

Tony sat watching her.

"Dolores, were you like in a rush to get home or something?"

Dolores looked at him slightly baffled. "Not really, why?"

"I mean if you feel like it, you wanna get some coffee?"

Dolores made a face, showing she was just a little uncomfortable.

"I'm just bored," he said with a smile.

"Tony, why don't you just go home to your wife?"

"She went to Hawaii. She left two days ago."

"Why didn't you guys just wait and go together?" Tony sat there with a lost expression saying nothing. "Aren't you goin' on vacation this week?"

"She didn't wanna wait, so she took her mom—on me of course—but it's cool. I'm just gonna meet them there Saturday." Dolores could see that he was bothered by it.

"Oh, that's cool." Dolores paused. "As long as you get there, right?" Dolores smiled.

"Yeah, I guess."

"Well, if you still wanna get some coffee, I'll go with you. I got a taste for a coffee cake."

Tony smiled.

◖◗◖◗

Dolores and Tony sat at the coffee shop. Soft music played in the background. Tony looked like a man taking down each issue of his life with every sip of his coffee.

"I appreciate you comin' out here with me, feelin' all sorry for me."

"It's no problem, no problem at all." They laughed.

"I just didn't feel like being alone tonight."

"Trust me, I know about being alone."

"So have you heard from what's his name?" Tony asked.

"He calls a couple times a week, but I don't answer. Thank God for caller ID."

"I think things happen for a reason," Tony said.

"Are you religious?" Dolores asked.

"Not really, but I definitely believe in God."

"Sometimes I don't understand what God is doing with my life. I think more than anything, all I've ever wanted was a family, and that just seems like something that's not gonna happen."

"Please. You'll have your own family someday."

"That's what everyone says."

"Maybe because it's true."

"Well, I hope someone proves me wrong."

"Trust me, it'll happen."

"You really think so?"

"What's the guy's name?"

"Mmm, Brad."

"Well let me just tell you this. He is a fool."

"A fool," Dolores repeated, amused and impressed by Tony's straightforwardness.

"That's the only way to describe any man who loses a woman who is as special and kind as you. I mean, damn, you're the complete package."

Dolores blushed. "Okay stop. You makin' me feel like you're tryin' to stop me from jumpin' off a bridge or somethin'." They laughed.

"Dolores, can I ask you a personal question?"

"It depends on what it is."

"Maybe I shouldn't ask."

"Look, you brought it up, now spit it out. If I don't wanna answer it, trust me I won't."

"And you won't get offended?"

"I can't say I won't get offended, but I'll tell you this, I won't take it personal," Dolores said with a smile. Tony's expression turned serious.

"Just keep in mind it's just what I heard." Tony paused. "Are you a virgin?" Dolores burst out laughing.

"You said it so seriously. I thought you were gonna ask me am I dying or something."

Tony laughed a little. "Well, I didn't mean to say it like that."

"Well, yeah, I'm a virgin."

"Oh, that's cool," Tony said with a look of concern.

"That's cool? Is that all you have to say?" Dolores chuckled.

"What do you want me to say?" Tony smiled, letting a laugh slip out.

"I don't know. What you're thinking, how? Why? Wow!" They laughed. "Well since we're talking all about my personal life, tell me a little bit about yours."

"What's there to tell? Married guy, hard worker, I don't know. What do you wanna know?"

"I don't know." Dolores took a bite of her coffee cake. "Well, how is it being married?" Tony took a moment, thinking as if he were on Jeopardy.

"Hard."

Dolores looked baffled.

"What?" Tony asked, reading the bewilderment on her face.

"Nothing," Dolores replied.

"I guess I've always wanted that family life, too, but it just doesn't seem all that it's cracked up to be," Tony said, really thinking about what he was saying.

"Well you gotta work on it sometimes."

"Yeah, but sometimes you gotta know when to quit. Otherwise you go through the rest of your life miserable, and life's definitely too short for that." They continued to talk until the coffee shop closed.

# TWENTY-TWO

Dolores stirred awake, staring at the ceiling. The digital clock on her nightstand read 3:05AM. She realized she had been awakened by the wetness between her legs. And her horniness would not go away if she did not do something about it. She sighed. She wanted to go back to sleep, but was unable to. She started to slowly caress her breast, trying her best to think about David, the guy from the beach. But Tony kept popping into her head. Dolores rubbed her breast harder, pinching her nipples. Then started to rub her legs together, feeling her vagina warming up and becoming even more wet. Her right hand slid down her chest to her stomach, then further down over her curly hairs to her vagina. She squeezed her vagina, letting her middle finger slide inside just a little. She exhaled.

She massaged her clitoris, taking her time, enjoying herself, staring at the ceiling. It was now 3:30AM.

The more she tried to think about David, the more she thought about Tony.

Suddenly, her eyes rolled up in the back of her head and her belly started to tremble, going up and down, violently vibrating back and forth until she came. Hard. "Ahhhhh!" A tear rolled out of the corner of her eye, partly from the orgasm and partly from the guilt of masturbating to thoughts of a married man.

ꛃ ꛃ ꛃ ꛃ

Dolores' cousin Carrie was sound asleep in bed with her husband. She jerked awake to the sound of the phone ringing. She looked at the clock on the wall, which read 7:52AM, then at her husband, who remained asleep. She snatched the phone off the nightstand. She was concerned because it was so early; everyone who knew her knew that she didn't wake up until at least ten. So naturally she thought something was wrong.

"Hello."

"Hello," the voice on the other end said.

"Hello, who is this?" Carrie asked, sitting up.

"It's me."

"Dolores?"

"Yeah."

"What's up, girl? Is everything okay?"

"Yeah, everything's fine. I'm sorry, did I wake you?"

"No. I was up. How's everything?" Carrie asked, wiping the sleep out of her eyes.

"Everything's okay.

"Girl, what's going on?" Carrie knew something was bothering Dolores. There was a pause on the other end.

"Nothin'."

"Dolores."

"Okay, I'm confused, girl!"

"About what?" Carrie knew that for Dolores to call her this early, she must really need to talk. And although they were extremely close back in the day, they had grown apart when Dolores moved to Los Angeles—and especially when Carrie got married. However, they could go without talking for as long as a year, but when they did talk, they didn't miss a beat. They would tell each other the most personal, intimate things. Their love was like that.

"I think I've fallen for the wrong guy."

"Who, Brad?"

"No."

"Who?" Carrie's eyebrows shot up. She got up and walked into the living room.

"A guy at my job." Dolores lay in bed rubbing her head. She had to talk to someone. She couldn't talk to Liz because she had a big mouth. But Carrie on the other hand was a good listener and gave great advice. "His name is Tony. And, girl he's married," Dolores said, ashamed of herself.

Carrie put her hand over her mouth, shocked. "Oh my God! And when did all this happen?"

"I don't know. Over the last couple of months. I mean, he is such a great guy."

"Have you done anything with him?"

"Of course not. He's married," Dolores snapped back. "But I did just have a hell of a dream about him."

Carrie heard the guilt in her voice.

"Girl, you were startin' to worry me."

"C'mon now, it's me. You know I don't get down like that." Dolores paused. "I just don't know if I'm on the rebound or what." She sighed, thinking about her feelings, searching for the truth. She wondered, was she really in love with Tony or was this about her being lonely and missing Brad? "But Carrie, this man has such a great heart. He's so funny, and smart, and handsome."

"I hear you. I mean, I think all women fantasize about men they can't have. That's totally natural. Don't beat yourself up too bad over a little dream." She smiled. "Hell, I fantasized about another man while I was having sex with my husband."

"Are you serious?"

"Yeah. Shoot. I be like, do your thing, Will! Get jiggy with it."

"Will Smith?"

"That's right."

They laughed. They talked for about an hour, laughing and sharing stories about former crushes. Carrie finally brought the conversation to a close.

"Girl, you crazy," Carrie said. "Dolores, don't worry about it, it's normal. We all have little crushes here and there. Just don't act on them and it's all good."

"You sure?"

"Yeah. Now go on to sleep, girl. I know it must be almost six in the morning out there."

"Yeah, all right; I'll talk to you sometime later this week."

"All right, sleep tight."

"Bye."

Dolores hung up the phone. She lay back in bed and closed her eyes. She tried to go to sleep, but she kept thinking about Tony, and what Carrie had said. She thought about how Tony was becoming a real friend, and not just a co-worker. And how it was okay to be attracted to him, as long as they didn't act on it. She smiled and drifted into a deep sleep.

TWENTY-THREE

Brad got up and went for his morning jog. He ran a park trail in Fox Hills, passing everyone in his path. It was a winding trail that went up and down as it formed a circle. He ran it hard, wanting to feel the pain in his legs as he pushed himself to exhaustion.

He was still kicking it with Nina, the girl he got caught with, but she was not the one for him and he knew it. For one thing she was too demanding—and everything was always about her. Plus, he was more attracted to Dolores, and the thought of what it would be like to make love to her was killing him. He felt like he put in all that work and some other brotha was going to reap all the benefits. And although he hated the fact that they were not having sex, it intrigued him that he would have been her first. He loved Dolores, and he knew that deep in her heart she loved him.

When he got home, he walked straight to the kitchen and poured a big glass of ice-cold water. His t-shirt was drenched with sweat and stuck to his body. He took it off and threw it on the washing machine. Suddenly, his doorbell rang. He dropped his head. "Shit."

When he opened the door, Nina stood there wearing tight jeans and a tighter blouse.

"Mmm," Nina said, pleased by the sight of Brad's sweaty chest and stomach muscles.

"Didn't I tell you to call before you come over? Damn!"

"I don't have to call."

"Yes, you do."

"No, I don't." She grabbed him by the hand and led him to his bedroom. "C'mon baby, I'm gonna lick the sweat off of you."

"You know you crazy, right?"

"That's why you love me. Besides, I don't see you fighting me." She pushed Brad onto the bed. His eyes glazed over as if he was under her spell. And he was. The sex was that good and nasty and he loved it.

 **TWENTY-FOUR**

Dolores stood in front of the theater desperately scanning the streets. Her watch read 8:00PM. Her eyes showed disappointment. Suddenly, Tony came running from around the corner.

"Dolores!"

"Hey! Hurry up, it's starting!" Dolores handed Tony a ticket and they dashed inside.

Tony and Dolores got to their seats just as the house lights went down. "We made it just in time," Dolores whispered.

"I'm just glad I called you," Tony said.

"Yeah, you caught me just as I was walking out of my house."

"Well, thanks for letting me tag along."

"No problem."

"Here." Tony handed Dolores a twenty-dollar bill.

"What's that for?"

"My ticket."

"That's all right, I got it." Dolores waved off his money.

"You sure?" Tony sat there holding the twenty-dollar bill.

"Put that away!" Dolores smiled at Tony, then turned her attention to the movie. Tony put his money back in his pocket, but his eyes remained fixed on Dolores. Dolores looked straight ahead but could tell Tony was staring at her.

Tony and Dolores strolled through the parking lot, admiring the beautiful night and the stars that lit it.

"So, what are you gonna do now?" Tony asked.

"Just go home, I guess."

"Let me ask you a question," Tony said, getting serious.

"What, am I still a virgin?" They both gave a little laugh.

"No. I wanna ask, do you think women cheat as much as men?"

"Why are you asking me?" Dolores laughed.

"You are a woman, aren't you? So, do they?"

"Well, let me see. Of course they do. Women are just better liars. But they just don't cheat with the same intensity and stupidity that men do," Dolores said playfully.

"Wow."

"Why? You think Mary might be foolin' around?"

"Who knows. Probably. She fits the profile: deceitful, conniving as hell. But the funny part about it is, I really don't care."

"Yes you do—you just don't wanna care. I mean, if you think she's cheatin' just ask her and see how she responds."

"You don't get it. I really just don't care anymore."

"Tony, I'm telling you as a friend, you do." Dolores gave Tony a quick hug and got in her car. "Goodnight, Tony. And talk to your wife."

"All right," Tony said. He waved as she drove off.

Dolores drove home thinking about Tony and what was happening to them. And what boundaries they would cross if they continued to be friends. She saw the way he was staring at her in the theater, and she knew that they were getting too close. She made up her mind that night that she would keep their relationship strictly professional. No more movies or drinks after work. She knew it was the best thing for both of them.

꾸ꆼꒊꋫ

When Tony got home, all of the lights were on and the television was blaring. He had rushed out of the house trying to get to the theater on time, and forgot to turn off everything. He even forgot to close the back door. "Shit," he said to himself as he shut the door.

Tony entered his bedroom and threw himself on his big soft bed. He was tired. He had been working tremendously hard lately and didn't even realize it. Probably because he preferred being at work over being at his own home.

He stretched out in his bed taking up more space then usual and closed his eyes. They didn't stay closed for long. He picked up the phone to call Dolores. He had a question about work. Then he looked at the clock on the nightstand. It read 11:45 PM. He hung up the phone, not wanting a phone call about work to be mistaken for something else. Their relationship was already getting complicated. Tony lay back and thought about his life, and what was becoming of it.

He knew that he and Mary were growing apart. Like two people who had forgotten how to be friends. All they had left was mediocre sex and the common goal of accumulating more things. Cars, houses, clothes, jewelry. All the material desires of two ambitious people living in Los Angeles.

The only thing they had in common lately was the time they spent together looking at bigger houses than the one they just bought. They figured that one day they would buy a house in a gated community with at least five bedrooms, a bigger pool, and more grass in the backyard for when they had kids.

He wanted kids, but she told him that they needed to wait until he got a promotion. However, when he finally got that promotion, kids were not even brought up. Getting a bigger house was. He was making more than three hundred thousand a year. And Mary had a catering business that she was proud of, that generated an additional seven thousand a year to the pot. Mary figured that justified looking at two-million-dollar homes. But moving was the last thing on Tony's mind—especially in Los Angeles, where a half-million-dollar house was just a two-bedroom starter home.

He gave a little laugh, thinking his wife was definitely delusional. He refused to stress himself out over some big-ass house he could not afford, and Mary just looking at him like, 'handle it big daddy.' "Hell no," he said to himself. He could imagine her thinking that by adding her seven grand for that year, she was doing her part. And then he thought about how much child care would be—'cause lord knows, she wouldn't be up to the challenge of being a full-time mom.

He could hear her now, well I got meetings all day, and I need to do some consulting, oh I've got to finish this proposal. He shook his head thinking. "Thank God I don't have kids with this woman." He sighed. "What am I gonna do?" He loved her, but everything was different, she was not the girl he met in college, who he had saw dancing on a table at a fraternity party. Care-free and looking for the next adventure.

She ran track, pledged a sorority, went to Clark University in Atlanta on an exchange program for one year. Changed her major six times, finally settling on pre-law. She was influenced by the OJ trial, but once she got out of school and talked to some real lawyers she found out that the majority of their work isn't in the courtroom or on TV, but reading briefs. Lots and lots of briefs. She changed her mind and started her own catering company, getting a few jobs a year. She also started other business ventures, such as a music label, managing singers and actors, financial adviser, public relations firm, and the last one—the one that always made Tony laugh a little—life coach "slash" career consultant. She helped people find their passion and get them focused, to pursue their dreams. All of these businesses led nowhere.

He knew that what she really wanted was a rich husband who could afford to pay for all of her little business ventures. She would often say with a great amount of pride, "I refuse to work for anyone. I'm my own woman." He thought that was easy to say, when he was footing the bill. However, she was supportive of his career and what he was doing, so he always supported her in return.

She had changed, and so had he. He realized it wasn't about the house they lived in or the car they drove. It was about how they felt about themselves and each other. He wanted a family. He was thirty-three, and understood that life was short. And no one was going to love you more because you had a big house or an expensive car. At least no one who mattered.

# TWENTY-FIVE

Dolores was in her office sitting at her desk reading Tony's manuscript. She gave a little laugh and continued to read. Hearing a knock on the door, Dolores shoved the manuscript in a drawer. "Come in," she said.

Tony stepped inside wearing a big smile. "Hey."

"Oh, it's you. Close the door." Dolores pulled the manuscript out of the drawer.

"What do you think?"

"I like it." Dolores smiled, amused by Tony's eagerness.

"Now c'mon, I want you to be honest. Is it good?"

"If it wasn't, I wouldn't be at my job sneakin' to read it," Dolores replied. Tony smiled. Dolores giggled. "Yeah, it's pretty funny."

"It is, isn't it," Tony replied, beaming.

"Real funny," Dolores said. Tony walked over beside Dolores.

"What page are you on?"

"Ninety-one."

"Well keep reading; it gets better."

"Does your wife know that you based a character on her?"

"Huh?"

"You know, you call her "the bitch.""

"That's not necessarily based on her," Tony said with a straight face. Dolores smirked. She flipped to a page and started to read.

"Mary is a school teacher who looks very innocent and conservative; however, she is a real bitch."

Tony gave a guilty smile. "Let's just say she inspired the character."

"At least change the name! Damn! Has she read this?"

"No, she thinks it's a waste of time."

Tony smiled, but Dolores could see the hurt in his eyes. She waved Tony off with a smile.

"Well leave so I can finish it!"

"All right, but hurry up. Bently has some kind of announcement to make."

"All right," she said. After Tony walked out, Dolores continued to read. She loved it.

⌐⌐⌐⌐

Bently, Dolores, Tony, and nine other men and women sat around an oblong table in the main conference room.

"Is everyone here?" Bently asked.

"Everybody's here," Tony answered.

"All right. Just got off the phone with Richard Rhodes. He is the president of our company out in New York, as you all know. Basically, there's two positions open, and they're the same as Tony's job—same pay, same everything. It's an excellent opportunity." Bently paused for effect. "I recommended Dolores and Bob for the job. Congratulations!" Everyone applauded. Co-workers patted Dolores and Bob on the back. Everyone looked happy except for Tony. "So if you guys want the job, it's there for the taking."

"Oh, wow, that's great. But when do they want us?" Dolores asked, a little overwhelmed.

"That's the thing. If you guys take the jobs, you have to be there by Monday."

"That's only four days," Bob said.

"That's the way it goes sometimes," Bently replied. Bob and Dolores exchanged smiles. Dolores looked at Tony. He was trying to smile, but couldn't hide his disappointment. "I just want you guys to know we will miss you. And after today just take the rest of the week off and get ready for New York. Congratulations, you guys." Everyone applauded. Dolores smiled but was distracted by the displeasure in Tony's face. That night she felt like God intervened and separated the two of them for their own good. She felt a great sense of relief—a tough decision had been made for her.

◻◻◻◻

Tony came home carrying a bag of CDs for his trip and a couple of books. He was depressed and burned out. He grabbed his suitcase, turned off all the lights, locked the doors, and headed to his car.

He spent the drive to the airport thinking about the trip he was about to go on, but even more about how, when he returned, Dolores would be gone. He felt a deep sadness. He then thought about Mary. Was it true love? Could love for someone be measured he thought, or was this something that he was feeling because his relationship with Mary was on the rocks?

As he drove down Century Boulevard he saw the entrance road to LAX. He thought about Mary, then Dolores. A little smile crept across his face. He gripped the steering wheel tightly. He checked his rearview mirror and paused for a moment to stare at his own reflection. His mind was going, and his eyes showed it.

The one thing that Tony knew, was that a friendly hug in the office hallway was not going to be his last encounter with Dolores. He made a quick U-turn and punched it to Dolores'.

On the way he stopped at a newsstand and grabbed an *LA Weekly*. He leafed through the entertainment section. Smiled. Then glanced at his watch. It read 8:25PM. He hopped into his car and drove off.

囗囗囗囗

Dolores was packing her things when she heard a knock on the door. She looked through the peephole and saw Tony waiting patiently. Dolores opened the door slowly.

"Hey," Tony said with a smile.

"What are you doin' here? I thought you were going to Hawaii."

"Yeah, I know. I just thought I'd wait until, maybe tomorrow."

Dolores smiled. "Come in."

Tony strolled into the living room, looking at the empty boxes on the floor.

"I'm just tryin' to get my things organized and pack a few things."

"Want some help?" Tony asked.

"Yeah. Help me carry this box out of the room." Tony followed Dolores in her bedroom and helped her carry out a few boxes.

Tony ended up helping Dolores with most of her things. When they were done Tony sat on the floor, pooped.

"You want something to drink?" Dolores offered.

"Yeah. Watcha got?"

"Soda, orange juice, water."

"I'll take water."

Dolores went to the kitchen and returned with water. She sat down next to Tony.

"Here you go."

"So how do you feel about leaving?"

"I guess I'm okay with it."

"Have you ever been to New York before?"

"Sure. Well, when I was a kid, I used to go down there with my mom and dad."

"I've been out there a few times recently. It's nice. You'll like it."

"You think so?"

"Yeah." They share a smile.

"So where has this nice guy been hiding for the past two years?"

Tony laughed. "What are you talkin' about?"

"You were an asshole."

"Asshole?" he repeated, amused.

"Yes. Ask Liz. I hated you." They laughed.

"Well, I didn't mean to be."

"So what time does your flight leave for Hawaii?"

"Tomorrow at three." There was an uncomfortable silence, then Dolores smiled.

"I just wonder. When I leave, how you guys gonna get along without me?"

"Please! Ain't nobody gonna be thinking about you."

"You guys gonna be crying like babies—especially Liz."

"Yeah, we might miss you a little bit. I don't know about the crying stuff. But we will miss you," Tony admitted. Dolores and Tony gazed into each other's eyes.

"So what are your plans? You need to try to sell that book. It's good."

Tony smiled. "Maybe so."

"I'm gonna miss you," Dolores said. They stared at each other not saying anything.

"Well, I guess I should leave."

"Yeah, it's getting late." They got up and hugged. The hug was a little longer than usual, and definitely more intimate. They walked to the front door and Dolores opened it for Tony.

"I just wanna say, you've been a great friend," Tony said.

"You have too," Dolores replied.

They embraced again and looked like they enjoyed the hug a little too much. Dolores slowly pushed Tony out and closed the door. She then leaned against the door.

"I gotta get the hell outta LA. Quick."

TWENTY-SIX

Liz and Dolores sat in the park sitting on a bench watching some kids play. One kid was running from his mother, driving her absolutely crazy as she chased him ready to go. "Timothy, will you come here!" the woman yelled, stressed out. The kid continued to scramble away from his mom.

"See, that's exactly why I don't want no kids," Liz said.

"I think it's beautiful having kids, watching them grow up."

"Please. Look at that mother over there about to have a nervous breakdown 'inshit," Liz said laughing.

Dolores laughed, then a calm smile came over her. "I think it's beautiful."

They continued to watch as the stressed-out mother chased her child around the park.

"I'm gonna miss you, girl," Liz said, resting her head on Dolores' shoulder.

"I'm gonna miss you too." They held hands.

"Just look at it this way—now you got a reason to come to New York."

"Yeah, I heard they got some fine-ass men out there."

"And I'm sure you'll meet every one of them."

"You know it. I guess we'll have to work on you gettin' laid out in New York." They laughed.

"I'm not rushin' it. It'll happen when it's meant to happen. Plus, I wanna be in love when I do it."

"Shoot, all that time you and Tony been spending together, you should be..."

"Liz! Don't even go there. He's a friend, plus he's married."

"Girl, please. Everyone sees the way you two be lookin' at each other."

"And how is that?"

"I don't know. Like you guys admire the hell out of each other."

"And that's what you think?"

"That's what I see," Liz said.

⊔⊓⊔⊓

That night Dolores was in the bathtub with the music on when the doorbell rang. She dried off a little then wrapped a big white towel around her and headed to the front door. She figured it was Liz. When she opened the door, Tony stood there looking handsome, wearing slacks and a button-down. He was taken aback by the sight of her glistening body in a towel.

"Tony!" Dolores said, surprised.

"Hey."

"I thought you left this morning."

"I decided that I'm not in a rush to get there."

"What about Mary?"

"When I told her I wasn't coming out there, she actually sounded happy."

"Why aren't you going?" Dolores asked.

"I'd just rather stay out here."

A smile crept across Dolores' lips. "Well come in."

Tony stepped inside and Dolores raced back to the bathroom. Tony sat down on the sofa. "So what were you doin'?" Tony shouted.

"What does it look like? I was in the tub!" Dolores shouted back.

"Are you about to go somewhere?"

"No."

"Well, take your time." Tony crossed his leg over his knee. "Would you mind if I took you somewhere?"

"Where?" Dolores shouted back, unsure.

"Don't worry about it. You'll see."

"Hmm, a surprise ey'?"

"Yeah. Just finish taking your bath." Tony smiled.

Dolores was laying back in the tub wearing a smile as well. A curious smile. She began to sing while using her washcloth to slowly rub her arms, breasts, and legs. Tony sat back listening to Dolores. Her voice was raspy but beautiful. Tony's smile grew and grew.

ⵣⵣⵣⵣ

Dolores and Tony took their seats at the Kodak Theater, excited. "This is so sweet. I've been wanting to see this play for the longest."

"Yeah I know. I remember you said you liked Shakespeare."

The curtain went up and the play began.

Dolores and Tony watched intently as Romeo and Juliet faced their inevitable deaths, Dolores ended up in tears, and Tony's eyes were glazed over. When the curtain came down, they sat there in awe. The audience erupted in applause. "That was amazing," Dolores said.

"Damn! Shakespeare's bad."

The performers came back out to take their curtain call. The audience rose, applauding even louder. Some were even stomping their feet.

卍卐卍卐

After the play they strolled on the Santa Monica Pier eating cotton candy. "I love the ocean, especially at night," Dolores said. They gazed out at the waves and the ships' lights in the distance.

"Yeah, it is beautiful," Tony said.

Dolores paused, swallowing hard. "Tony, what are we doin' out here?"

"I don't know."

They strolled to the edge of the pier.

"If I tell you something, will you promise not to look at me like some scumbag?"

"What?" Dolores asked, taking the conversation in stride.

"I just want to tell you that I like you. I like you a lot."

Tony couldn't even look at her. Dolores sighed, and her eyes went soft. She couldn't look at him either.

"I like you too," she said.

"So what do we do?"

Dolores thought about it for a moment.

"Nothing. Absolutely nothing," she replied.

Tony looked at Dolores. Her eyes ran from his and settled on the black ocean again.

"Life is funny," Tony said.

"Yep."

"I mean, are you happy?"

"Yeah, I guess," Dolores said.

"I mean, if you could have anything in the world, what would it be?"

Dolores peered into Tony's eyes, then turned away.

"What's wrong?" Tony asked.

"I don't know."

"Answer my question," Tony persisted.

"I guess I got everything a girl could want. Good family, good job, good friends. Why, what would you want?"

"Just someone to love me, I mean truly love me, and for me to love them back with that same intensity." Tony chuckled. "Like Romeo and Juliet, that's love. Someone you're willing to die for and who's willing to die for you." He paused. "Someone who's a part of your, you know, soul."

"Yeah, I guess I wouldn't mind that either," Dolores said.

They stared deep into each other's eyes. Tony moved in for a kiss. Dolores stopped him just before their lips touched.

"I'm sorry, I shouldn't have done that," Tony said.

"It's okay. It's just, you know."

"Yeah. C'mon, let's go." They turned to leave, and Brad and Nina were walking straight toward them. Dolores looked like she had been sucker punched.

Tony read her expression. "What's wrong?"

A nervous Brad and a snobbish Nina were only a few feet away. Brad tried to avoid Dolores but could not. They were all too close.

"Hey, Dolores," Brad said. The tension between them was obvious.

"Hey," Dolores replied.

"So, how's everything goin'?" Brad asked.

"It's been goin' really good," Dolores answered. Dolores did a double-take at the sight of Nina, realizing she had seen her before. "Have I met you before?"

"Well you might have seen me over Brad's," Nina said wearing a condescending smile. Dolores thought about it and realized that this was the woman who passed her on the stairs in Brad's apartment building, the day she caught him cheating. Dolores shot Brad a look, holding her anger in check with a slight smile.

"So, how long have you guys been together?" Dolores asked. Nina loved every bit of this, wearing a wicked smile on her face.

"Oh, about eight months," Nina said with a smirk. Dolores gave Brad another evil glare. He stood there looking guilty. Tony saw what was going on.

"Well, that's cool. 'Cause me and my baby been together about five months, mostly on the down low," Tony added. He put his arm around Dolores, and kissed her on the cheek. Brad shrugged Tony off, knowing he was lying.

"Can I talk to you for a second?" Brad asked Dolores. Dolores thought about it for a moment, then nodded "yes", while Nina stared at Brad with an attitude. Brad shot Nina a quick glance, ignoring her attitude.

The two of them walked a good distance away. Nina smiled at Tony, trying to mask her anger. The two of them stood there, sizing each other up.

"So Dolores is your woman now, huh?" Nina asked in a patronizing tone.

"Yep," Tony answered, hands in his pockets.

"Honey, you shouldn't even waste your time. Brad said she ain't nothin' but a tease."

Tony smiled. "That's cool, that's how I like em'."

"Is that right?"

"Yeah, I like to work for it, 'cause I can't stand those kinda ho's who just be sleepin' around like their coochies are going to go bad if they don't use it every chance they get. You know the kinda tramps I'm talkin' about?" Tony said.

Nina stood there dumbfounded.

Dolores and Brad stood silent. They both stared at the water. It was the perfect excuse not to look at each other. "So how you been doin'?" Brad asked.

"Good."

"Look, I just wanted to say I'm sorry."

"Me, too," Dolores said.

"For what?" Brad asked, surprised.

"I don't know. I just felt like I owed you that too."

"Did you get my letters?"

"Yeah."

"So what did you think?"

"I don't know; I never read them."

"Oh. Well, I kinda figured that," Brad said. His eyes begged for forgiveness. "I thought Tony was married."

"He is. I'm just leaving for New York tomorrow, taking a new job, and he took me to a play."

"You're leaving?"

"Four o'clock sharp," Dolores said. Brad stared at her, dumbfounded. He shook the confused expression off of his face trying to act unfazed.

"Since when did you guys become all buddy-buddy? I thought you hated him."

"Well I did, but he turned out to be a nice guy. They made us start working together, and I guess we became, you know, friends."

"That's cool," Brad said suspicious of the way she said *friends*. "I fucked up, huh?"

"I don't know. Maybe it just wasn't meant to be."

"Or maybe we didn't give it a chance."

His words hit Dolores hard. She looked at Tony and Nina, taking turns between looking at the water and looking over at them.

"Maybe," Dolores said. "But I've moved on, and I'm moving to New York. You've moved on, obviously, so it is what it is."

"You don't think we could maybe see each other again? See what happens?"

"To be honest, no. I got enough drama going on in my life."

"Well, can you do me at least one favor?"

Dolores stared back at him.

"Read my letters."

Dolores thought about it for a moment. "All right."

"Can I at least have a hug since you're going to New York?" Brad opened his arms for a hug.

"No," Dolores said without missing a beat. They each gave a little laugh.

"Well, that's fair."

◧◨◧◨

Tony and Dolores approached her front door late that night. Dolores was still shook up from seeing Brad, but happy to be in the company of Tony.

"Well, this is it," Dolores said.

"Yeah, I know."

"Thank you for a wonderful night."

"It was my pleasure."

"Well," Dolores said. Their eyes were locked.

"All right. You have a safe trip, all right?" Tony gave Dolores a quick hug and headed off.

"Tony," Dolores called out. Tony reeled around, looking somber. "I just want you to know, I really hate the fact that you're married." They smiled.

"Me, too."

Dolores used her index finger to call him to her. Tony swallowed hard and slowly walked to her, their eyes locked once again. Dolores gave him a soft kiss on the cheek. Then she waved good-bye. Tony smiled, then turned and walked away.

TWENTY-SEVEN

The next day Dolores and Liz stacked boxes. "Just leave that there, I'll get it," Liz said, grabbing another box.

"What time is it?" Dolores asked. Liz checked her watch.

"Twelve o'clock."

"Yeah, let me go get the rest of my stuff." Dolores marched into her bedroom, then came back out carrying two large suitcases. "So, you're gonna stay here and wait for the movers, right?" Dolores set the two suitcases by the door.

"Yeah, don't worry about it. I got it."

"Remember, tell them to be careful with my china."

"I said I got it."

The front door was open and the driver peeked his head inside. "Ms. King?"

"Yeah, come in," Dolores said, gathering her things. "You can take those two suitcases."

He grabbed the two suitcases and headed out.

"You got everything?" Liz asked.

Dolores held her purse and a few of her bags. "Yeah," she said with sad eyes.

"I'm gonna miss you so much," Liz said, making a boo-boo face.

"I'm gonna miss you too, girl." They embraced tightly, both of them very close to tears.

"That's all right. You know I'm still gonna call you all the time," Liz said. Dolores smiled. "Collect, of course."

Dolores gave a little laugh. "I wouldn't expect you to call any other way. All right, girl." They continued to hug each other.

"You have a safe trip, all right?" Liz said.

"I will."

They stopped hugging. Dolores took a final look around her apartment then walked out.

Liz watched her best friend leave then she stacked the remaining boxes. The phone rang. Liz ignored it for a moment, but finally she put down the box she was holding and strolled to the phone. It was Tony, calling from his backyard.

"Hello?" Tony said, sounding stressed.

"Uh, who's callin'?" Liz asked.

"Is this Liz?"

"Yeah."

"This is Tony."

"Oh, hey Tony."

"Hey, uh, can I talk to Dolores for a second?"

"She just left."

Tony paused for a moment. "Do you know when she'll be back?"

"She's gone to New York."

"I thought her flight didn't leave til' four."

"She got an earlier flight."

"How long ago did she leave?"

"She just left."

"Oh."

"Is anything wrong?" Liz asked.

"No, nothing's wrong. All right, I'll see you later then," Tony said, trying to hide his feelings. He hesitated for a moment, then called Dolores' cell phone. There was no answer.

The driver drove like a wild man, while playing very loud disco music. Dolores shook her head as he sung along. "This is my song," he said. She nodded as if she couldn't care less. Over the music and bad singing, she could not hear her cell phone ringing.

She looked dejected, thinking about where she was going and what she was leaving behind. She knew that she was doing the right thing. She was in love with a married man, and knew that this job could not have come at a better time. She thought to herself that she would go to New York, take over the company, meet a great man, get married, and live happily ever after.

Tony sat in his backyard, cordless phone in hand, thinking about Dolores and what Liz told him. Suddenly, he popped up and sprinted into the house.

The driver pulled up in front of the airline and got Dolores' suitcases out of the trunk. She tipped the driver, amazed by his unprofessionalism, then signaled a skycap to get her suitcases.

Tony drove like a man possessed. He didn't know what he was going to say once he saw her, but he knew he had to see her. It was at that moment that Tony realized he had fallen in love. And the thought of not being able to see Dolores made him physically ill. Dolores appreciated his mind and heart, and he knew it. She made him believe that being in love could be easy, and that it did not have to be emotionally draining. He knew that with her he could accomplish anything. Most of all true happiness.

Dolores was in line to board the plane. She continued to think about Tony. She knew they were getting too close, and that eventually they would cross a line that they would regret later. In her heart she knew they already had.

Tony's car came to a screeching halt in front of the airport. He jumped out and ran past a security guard.

"Hey, you can't park there!" the security guard shouted.

"Just give me a ticket!"

Tony rushed into the airport frantically looking for Dolores. He ran to the schedule board and saw Delta LA to NEW YORK at one o'clock. He looked at his watch. It was 12:50PM. He ran off at full speed.

The stewardess was closing the doors to Dolores' flight. Tony turned the corner running and realized that he was too late. He came to a stop and bent over, trying to catch his breath.

Tony walked out of the terminal dragging his feet, head down. He looked up in time to see his car being towed down the street. His expression was priceless. His expression became even more priceless when he saw Brad running across the street, looking as desperate as he did.

❧ ❧ ❧ ❧

Dolores stared out the window as the plane took off. She reclined her seat and reached into her purse. She pulled out a bundle of letters. All from Brad. She hesitated before opening one. She stared out the window again looking at the clouds as the plane rose. She opened the letter.

Dear Dolores,

Hey baby, I don't know what to say. All I know is that I fucked up bad. I hope when you read this you'll understand that I'm not trying to convince you to forget what I did, but just understand that I'm only human, and I made a mistake. I love you, and I want you back so bad. I know you still love me. Come on babe, give me a call, or at least take my call. I made a mistake. I don't know why I did it. Maybe because I felt like I couldn't wait, and as bad as it sounds, I was using her almost like a crutch. She was a pain in the ass. I mean sometime I felt like I didn't even like her. But she satisfied me sexually. You were the one I loved. So it seemed perfect. I feel stupid being this honest. I'm sure you're gonna tear this up and never give me another chance. But, I do want you to know that I was going to write you some bullshit about how it was a person I slept with once, and how I did it because we weren't having sex. But I want to be honest. I've been sleeping with her for the last three months. She was down with sex even though I was engaged. But then she started to have feelings for me. I was going to tell her that day that it was over. But then you called. Talk about bad luck. You know I'm not good with words, but I figured if I told the truth, maybe you would see me for what I am, a man. I'm so sorry, please give me another chance.

Love, Brad

▢ ▢ ▢ ▢

The next night Tony whipped up some chili in the kitchen, disheartened and still thinking about Dolores. Tony was a great cook, and liked to cook to relax. Suddenly, he looked up, hearing keys rattle in the front door and the doorknob turn. Mary stumbled in with her suitcases and bags. "I'm home!" she shouted.

Tony paused for a moment, then continued to stir his chili, face stoic, as Mary strolled in the kitchen wearing a huge smile. "Hey, didn't you hear me?"

"Yeah, I just don't want this stuff to burn," Tony said. Mary gave Tony a hug. He continued to stir his chili, leaning in for the hug. She could tell something was wrong.

"I missed you, so me and mom came back early."

"Is that right." Tony gave a smirk. "What's that, about twenty-four whole hours?"

"What's the matter with you?"

"Nothing."

"Oh, you mad 'cause I left without you?"

"No."

"I don't see what the problem is. You could've left with us."

"I had to work."

"Well, you didn't even come out when you were supposed to."

"Look, don't start no shit with me right now." Tony calmly continued to stir his chili while Mary stared at him. She could see that he was upset, but the fact that he was being so cool about it made her uneasy.

"Look, I'm sorry for whatever I did."

"That's the problem. You don't know what you did, do you?"

"Well, damn, tell me what I did then." Mary said with an attitude.

"Just leave me alone."

"This about me goin' to Hawaii? Damn, get over it already. Shit, if I tried to wait on your ass, I wouldn't have went at all."

"You are so full of shit," Tony said, showing his anger.

"I'm full of shit? You're full of shit!" Mary shouted.

"Don't make excuses. You left without me because you just couldn't wait, and didn't think about anyone else but yourself—like you always do—come in here eight days later, talkin' 'bout you miss me. Please!"

"Whatever."

"This is hopeless."

"What's hopeless?"

"Me and you," Tony said with contempt.

Mary stopped in her tracks. "Tony, what do you want me to say?" she asked, trying to calm things down.

"I just don't think this is gonna work," Tony said, holding his ground.

Mary paused, taking it all in, looking around almost as if she was looking for someone to come to her aid. She slowly approached Tony with puppy-dog eyes and a half smile. She slipped her arms around his waist, staring deep into his eyes.

"I'm sorry, okay? I'm sorry." Mary hugged Tony tightly, but he didn't hug her back. She kissed him on the lips, then gave slow kisses all over his face, seducing him with each one. Tony had a blank expression on his face, but he eventually gave in and kissed her back.

# TWENTY-EIGHT

Three months later Dolores was doing great. She was shuffling through her papers late one afternoon in her office when her cell phone rang. Dolores checked the caller ID and answered it. "Hey, what's up, girl?" she asked.

"Nothin'. Just up here sittin' at this desk," Liz said.

"So how's everybody?" Dolores asked as she continued to shuffle through the papers.

"Hmm, everyone's okay. Anything new goin' on out there?"

"Same ole same ole." Dolores paused.

"You still comin' out here in two weeks, right?" Dolores asked.

"Oh yeah, for sure."

"Well, let me get you back. I got a lot of work to do."

"All right, then. I'll talk to you later."

Dolores stopped what she was doing. "Hey, how's Tony doin'?"

"Doin' all right."

"Well, tell him I said… Never mind. Don't say nothin'. All right, girl, I'll talk to you later."

"All right." Liz sat back in her chair. She seemed sad.

Dolores hung up the phone and stared out of the massive window behind her desk. Gazing at the city lights of Manhattan, she zoned out thinking about her first week in New York.

🯲 🯲 🯲 🯲

Brad remained in the airport until he concluded that either Dolores lied to him or she caught an earlier flight. He called her house but got no answer so he went to the airport bar and drank and watched baseball until it closed.

He woke up the next morning stretched out on three seats in the airport lounge. A five-year-old boy holding a Spider Man action figure stared at him. Brad came to, not sure where he was. He got up and went to the restroom to wash his face. His cell phone rang. It was Nina. He shut off the ringer and put the phone away. After he brushed his teeth with his finger, he stared at himself in the mirror. "What am I doing?" he asked himself.

Back in the airport lounge, he called Dolores' job. A receptionist answered.

"Yeah, can I speak to Dolores King, please?" Brad asked, disguising his voice just in case Liz answered.

"She no longer works here."

"She's not there?"

"No, she moved to New York."

"Oh, okay." Brad hung up. "Fuck this."

Brad was on the airplane hung over, drinking coffee like water. He had no idea where he was staying, or what he was going to say to Dolores when he saw her. All he knew was that he had to see her and get her back. He loved her, and had to try to undo the biggest mistake of his life.

After he landed in New York, Brad got a room at a Motel Six. He got the address of Dolores' office and was going to go there that night, but it was getting late and he looked a mess.

The next morning he showered and shaved, putting back on the same clothes he wore the day before. He was nervous, but this was something he had to do. He arrived at noon, in the lobby of the high-rise and waited. He was pretty sure he was wasting his time, but he hoped he could catch Dolores going to lunch and they could talk. And soon enough she did. However, she was not alone.

Dolores was with a group of her co-workers. She saw him waiting in a chair by the double doors leading out into the streets. She was stunned. "Brad?"

"Hey."

"What are you doing here?"

"I came to see you."

She stood dumbfounded. "Can I talk to you for a moment?" Dolores ushered Brad away from her co-workers. "Brad, why are you really out here?"

"For you."

Dolores looked at her co-workers, who were waiting by the door talking to each other.

"Brad, this is a bad time. I'm going to lunch with my new co-workers."

"Okay. I don't wanna mess you up, I just want to talk to you. Maybe after work?"

Dolores hesitated, not really sure what to say. "All right," she said, hoping she wouldn't regret it.

"Okay. Cool."

"Okay."

"I'll meet you down here. What time?"

She thought for a moment. "Six."

"Okay, cool," Brad said, smiling.

Dolores returned his smile, but was taken a back by the ambush. She joined her co-workers, and left the building looking back at Brad amazed that he was there.

After work that night, Dolores strolled through the lounge. Brad stood by the door, looking like an eager doorman. Dolores was hesitant, and approached Brad wearing an uncertain smile.

"So where do you wanna go?" Brad asked.

"Well, I hear there's a great little coffee shop around the corner."

"Cool."

They left the building and walked around the corner to the twenty-four-hour coffee shop. Dolores picked a table in the back, out of the way. She figured if things got ugly she could tell Brad where to go without making too much of a scene.

They both were silent while they drank their coffee.

"So, Brad, what are you doing here?"

"I'm here because I love you."

"You love me?"

"Yeah."

"Brad, look. I don't know what we're doing here…"

"Why you trying to act like you don't love me anymore?"

"Because I don't."

"Dolores, why you lying?"

"I'm not."

"Yes, you are." Brad smiled. "How many times do I have to say, "I'm sorry?""

"You don't have to say I'm sorry. I'm over it. And frankly, I'm over you."

Their eyes were locked. A staring contest.

"Look, let's just be friends and see what happens."

"Friends?" Dolores repeated, almost amused.

"Yeah, friends," Brad said.

"What do you expect me to say? "Oh, Brad, it's all good. Let's get back together and live happily ever after!"

"Look, I'm out here and I'm trying." They stared at each other. "Dolores, I really am sorry."

"What about Nina?"

"What about her?"

Dolores gave him a look.

"Look, I'm talking about us, all right?"

"I hear you, but I really just don't know what to say."

"Say you'll be my friend."

"I don't know."

"C'mon, girl. Stop being so... hard."

"You made me this way."

"Well, damn, I'm sorry."

Dolores stared at him as if she was trying to read his mind. "I have to be up early, and I got a lot of work to do tonight. So, where are you stayin'?"

"Currently? In my rent-a-car."

Dolores knew that Brad wanted to stay with her. She took a moment, looking around the coffee shop, as she weighed the decision she was about to make.

"If you want, you can stay at my place." She paused. "On the couch of course."

A smile stretched across Brad's face.

"I'm serious as a heart attack. On the couch."

"That's cool."

"I'm only doin' this because my new apartment scares me."

"What's wrong with it?"

"It just looks kind of creepy. It belongs to the company. I'm staying there until I find a condo." Dolores asked herself, What have I just done? "This doesn't mean anything, Brad. Okay?"

"Yeah, it's cool."

Dolores' apartment was decorated like an old person or vampire lived there, with gaudy furniture and gold statues throughout the living room. It was not Dolores' style at all.

"Nice," Brad said looking around. He started to laugh.

She laughed as well. "Ha ha."

"I think I'm scared to stay here, too." They laughed.

"You want something to drink?"

"No, I'm cool." Brad took off his jacket while Dolores strolled into the kitchen.

"Well, I'm gettin' a glass of wine."

"In that case I'll take a glass of wine, too. I know how you don't like to drink wine alone."

Dolores smiled as she grabbed a bottle and two glasses. They sat at the dining room table. After she poured the wine, they sat looking at each other, not knowing what to say.

Dolores sipped her wine. "I love a good bottle of wine."

"I know." Brad said amused.

"Well, you poppin' up on a sista, done drove me to drinkin' on a weekday." Dolores downed her wine like it was water.

"You just gonna torture me all night, huh?"

"No. I got work to do tonight, and I got to be up early."

"I just want to say that I appreciate you talking to me." He downed his wine. "I made a stupid mistake."

Dolores relaxed and poured herself some more wine. "You know I read your letters."

"You did?"

"Yeah."

"I don't expect you to just jump back into my arms. I just want to be friends."

Dolores smiled. "Friends, huh?"

"Yeah."

"I could do that," Dolores said, with a sheepish grin.

Brad slowly slid his hands across the table and rested them on top of hers. Her grin ceased and a calm smile came over Brad's face. Dolores swallowed the lump in her throat, trying her best to look unaffected. She downed some more wine, as if it was the antidote to Brad.

That night they talked about everything. She told him about her escapades with Liz, and about being out on the club scene looking for sex. They laughed as she described each encounter—without going into too much detail. Brad told her what Nina was really like and how she was certifiably insane. And how she tried to claim she was pregnant while she was on her period. They laughed hysterically.

 **TWENTY-NINE**

Dolores continued to gaze out of her office window, thinking about her first week out there. She thought how funny life could be, not knowing what was around the corner.

Brad stayed with Dolores for two weeks, then they hopped in a rent-a-car and drove to DC. They showed up at her mom and dad's house while they were eating dinner. Jackie opened the door. "Oh my God! Dolores is here! Lenny, our baby's home!" Dolores and her mother hugged.

They gathered at the dining room table. Dolores' parents were beaming at their daughter, happy that she was with a man. "Mom, dad, Brad and I have something to tell you guys."

"What is it?" her mom asked. Her parents leaned forward, eager to catch the words as soon as they left her lips.

"We're getting married," Dolores said in a higher voice than usual.

Jackie screamed and hugged Dolores around the neck. Lenny stuck his hand out.

"Congratulations, Brad."

"Thank you sir." They shook hands as if they were solidifying a business deal.

Lenny got up and kissed Dolores on the forehead. "Congratulations, baby."

"Thank you, daddy."

Jackie hugged Brad. "I knew it when I saw you two at my door," she said with glee.

"No you didn't, mom."

"I did." She smiled at Dolores and Brad, who looked like two kids in love for the first time.

Dolores and Jackie sat on the couch talking while Lenny and Brad slept. Dolores lived for these late-night conversations with her mother. Dolores was glowing, excited that she would finally be getting married and making love for the first time. She thought about Tony, but he was married and now she was getting married as well. So that part of her life was officially over, and she felt great about it.

They didn't want a big wedding. They wanted it quick and beautiful, so they decided to have it in the Bahamas. The plan was to get married in six months.

When Liz heard the news she flipped out. She told Dolores not to marry Brad. She thought he was a creep, and that she was just doing it for the sake of being married. Dolores and Liz argued for weeks. Dolores was not trying to hear it, but at night, when she was in bed alone staring at the ceiling, she thought about what Liz said. She asked herself. Is it love or convenience? She thought that Liz might be a little jealous, losing her best friend to a man she could not stand. She never did like Brad, but she tolerated him because Dolores said she loved him. So when he got busted with another woman, Liz was happy. She never let Dolores know it, but she was.

"Are you going to be my bridesmaid or not?!" Dolores snapped.

"Of course I will, but I don't have to like it."

"What kind of shit is that? Look, I don't want that kind of energy at my wedding, so if you don't wanna be there, just let me know."

"Are you going to buy my ticket?"

Dolores looked into the phone like, No this bitch didn't! "Hello?" Liz continued.

"Yeah, Liz," Dolores said, too through with Liz and her attitude.

"Well, all right then, I'll be there," Liz replied.

"You a trip."

"Look, I just want what's best for you, girl, that's all."

"Then be happy for me."

There was a long pause on Liz's end. "Fine," Liz said.

"I'm serious, Liz."

"Okay."

"Good. You know I love you like a sister," Dolores added.

"I know," Liz said, shaking her head.

"So, you and Carrie are going to have to really help me get this thing together."

"I kind of figured that. How is Carrie, anyway?"

"She's good. I know she's working on havin' a baby."

"Mmm."

"What's that supposed to mean?" Dolores asked, irritated.

"Nothing."

"Well, anyway, I'll see you in the Bahamas."

"I'll be there," Liz said.

"Bye."

"Bye."

They both hung up, irritated with each other.

Liz lay in bed staring out of the window. She knew her best friend was about to make the biggest mistake of her life. And now she had a huge decision of her own to make. Whether or not to tell Dolores what happened the night she had too much to drink and Brad drove her home.

# THIRTY

Tony was in the office kitchen pouring a cup of coffee when Liz strolled in.

"Hey, Tony."

"Hey, Liz, how you doin'?"

"Fine."

"Haven't seen you in a while."

"I've been really busy," Liz said, grabbing some creamer.

"So, have you talked to Dolores lately?" Tony looked uncomfortable asking.

"Oh, yeah. I talked to her a couple of days ago. She's getting married, you know." Tony stopped pouring his sugar.

"Married? To who?"

"Brad. Her old fiancé."

"How'd that happen?"

"He went to New York and fought for her, I guess." She looked at Tony like he should have been the one to fight for her.

"Wow," Tony responeded involuntarily.

"But you know what? She's making a huge mistake," Liz said.

"Why do you say that?"

"Because he's a dog."

"Hey, who are we to judge?" Tony responded.

Liz rolled her eyes. "Yeah, you're probably right. Maybe she's just in love," Liz said. "Or just tired of waiting for Mr. Right."

They looked at each other for a moment.

"So, you don't think she really loves him?" Tony asked.

"What do you think, Tony?" Liz said as if they both knew. Dolores loved Tony, and now she was settling. "I'm going to the Bahamas next weekend so she can marry this dude."

"Next weekend!"

"Hey, they wanna do it as soon as possible."

"Did she at least sound happy?" Tony asked, stirring his coffee, almost becoming mesmerized by it.

"I don't know. What I do know is that she's marrying a pig. That I know for sure."

"You say that like you know something she doesn't."

"Well, she caught him cheating. What more do you want?"

Dolores and Brad were in bed in Dolores' apartment watching television almost in a trance. The nightly news showed a huge storm in the south that wiped out many homes and killed twelve people. "This is some deep shit," Brad said.

"I know. Man, one minute you're here, the next minute you're outta here."

"Ain't that the truth," Brad said.

"I just wanna get married, have some kids, be happy. Is that too much to ask? I just wanna be happy."

"All of that is about to come true." Brad smiled, in love.

"You think so?"

"I know so. I love you, Dolores."

"I love you, too." Dolores spoke the words but heard them like never before. An image of Tony jolted into her mind. She smiled at Brad. They both looked at the suitcases by the door.

"Is Liz still coming?"

"Yeah. I sent her a ticket."

"Why'd you have to send her a ticket?"

"She don't have money like that."

"Well, I would have made her ass walk—take a canoe or somethin'."

"She's my maid of honor."

"If it was her damn wedding, I bet she'd find a way!"

"Look, that's my girl. It's not a problem."

"Whatever."

"Why you don't like Liz?"

"Because she's a hater."

"She's not a hater."

"Yes she is. As soon as we got engaged, she was nothing but negative."

"She's just protective, that's all."

"Protective of what?"

"Protective of me."

"Hater."

"She's not a hater."

"I bet she didn't want you to marry me when you told her."

Dolores hesitated for a moment, thinking about what he was saying. "See, hater."

"Look, Liz has my back. Trust me on that. That I do know for sure."

THIRTY-ONE

A week after Dolores left for New York, Tony and Mary sat in the hospital lobby, waiting to see the doctor about getting pregnant.

Tony always wanted kids and was ready to start a family four years ago. But Mary refused to mess up her perfect body birthing babies. However, she'd had a change of heart. At thirty-four, she knew her clock was ticking—plus two of her running buddies were knocked up, so naturally she wanted to get pregnant as quick as possible.

Tony sat there in a daze thinking about what he was doing and who he was doing it with. Yes, Mary was his wife, but their relationship was changing. And it wasn't for the better. He knew deep in his heart that Mary was not his soul mate, and that his true soul mate was in New York City. "Mary, we gotta talk," Tony said, rubbing his forehead.

"What's wrong, honey? You scared?" Mary asked, smiling.

"I don't know."

"Look, it's natural to be a little scared about being a father."

"I'm not scared of being a father."

She looked at him as if he was lying. "It's okay. I know you are going to make a great dad."

"Do you even love me?" Tony blurted out.

"What?"

"You heard me. Do you love me?"

"Of course I love you."

"I think we need to talk about this before we go any further."

"Talk about what?"

"Getting pregnant."

"You gotta be kiddin' me." Mary looked at him with contempt.

"No I'm not," Tony shot back.

"Goddamn it! You just can't say 'yes baby'! Everything's gotta be such a damn thing with you."

"Why, because I'm not saying yes to you?"

"So what? You don't wanna have a baby?"

"Yes. I want a baby. I'm just not sure I wanna have one with you."

"What?" Mary looked confused for a moment, then her eyes filled with rage.

Tony sat stone faced. "You heard me."

"How could you say that to me? I'm your fucking wife."

"I know. I just need to think."

"Think about what, fool? You know I've been off birth control for a month and a half now, and I'm a week late. So what are you talking about?" Tony sighed.

"You're a week late?"

"Yeah. I figured we'd get tested while we're here. I wanted to surprise you."

Tony just looked at her, outdone.

ꗢ ꗢ ꗢ ꗢ

They stepped into the house, tired and frustrated. Mary stomped through the living room, and headed for the bedroom.

"Mary!" Tony shouted, exhausted from arguing for two hours straight.

"I have nothing to say to you!" Mary shot back.

Tony was going to respond but he held his tongue. He threw his keys on the coffee table and plopped on the sofa. He jumped when he heard the bedroom door slam shut.

Mary crawled in bed and started to cry. "What am I going to do?" she asked her-self. She thought about her future with the man on the couch in the living room and cried harder.

THIRTY-TWO

Dolores and Brad were on a plane to the Bahamas. Family and friends were on their way as well. Jackie, Lenny, Uncle Charles, Lilly, Steve the minister, Carrie and her husband Kevin all were headed to the Bahamas to see their favorite girl get married and over that broom.

꒡ ꒙ ꒡ ꒙

Brad and Dolores entered the penthouse suite. "Oh my God, look at this room!" Dolores rushed over to the huge window overlooking the resort. "And the view." Brad smiled as his beautiful woman pranced around the room. She opened the sliding glass door to the balcony and stepped outside, taking in the view.

"It's the best suite in the hotel," Brad said, taking in the view as well.

"Oh my God! I can't believe it's really going to happen. We are going to get married," Dolores said.

"I know," Brad replied.

Dolores hugged him, resting her head on his chest.

Brad gently stroked her head, running his fingers through her hair. "I just love you so much. And thank God you gave me a second chance."

"Well, if you didn't come to New York, we wouldn't be here. So thank you for not giving up." They kissed. Below them, hotel guests were out by the pool taking in the sun, swimming, and drinking at the bar. They rested their elbows on the balcony rail, looking down at the people coming and going.

"Is that Liz?" Brad's expression turned sour.

"Where?" Dolores asked.

"Right there. And who is she with?" Dolores continued to look, trying to pick out Liz. Brad suddenly stood up straight. "Is that Tony?"

"Tony?" Dolores looked harder, and her jaw dropped when she spotted Liz and Tony, carrying suitcases.

ठ ठ ठ ठ

Dolores and Liz stood face to face in Liz's room. "What the fuck are you smokin'?" Dolores asked, throwing her hands in the air.

"He wanted to come."

"This is my wedding! And you're trying to sabotage it!" Dolores shouted, pacing the room, holding her head like she had a terrible headache.

"I'm not tryin' to sabotage your wedding!"

"Well, what is it then? Are you hatin' or what?!"

"No, I'm not hatin'!" Liz snapped back, offended.

"Well then, why would you bring someone I'm in love with out here?" Dolores froze from her own words and so did Liz.

"See, I knew you loved him," Liz said touched.

"Love? Love who?" Dolores said stumbling over her words.

"Love Tony."

"As a person."

"Why you lying?"

"I'm not lying. I love Tony as a person, but I'm in love with Brad, my fiancé."

"Your fiancé is a dog. And I wouldn't be your best friend if I knowingly let you make one of the biggest mistakes of your life."

"I'm not making no damn mistake. And if you're not going to be supportive of me, getting married, then you need to just go."

"Well, Tony wants to talk to you."

"No. What he needs to do is go home with you and talk to his wife."

"They got divorced."

"Divorced?"

"Yeah. He wants you."

Dolores stood in shock for a moment. "Look, I'm marrying Brad tomorrow, so you and Tony can just leave. I don't know what your problem is, but if you're not going to be supportive, you need to go. Matter of fact, I want you to go."

"It's like that?" Liz said, arms folded.

"You made it like that." Dolores got even more emotional. "You know, even before I caught Brad cheatin', you were against him. I think you just got a problem with men. Maybe that's why you got so many of them. Hell, you got issues, girl." Liz looked like she had been cut to the bone. Her eyes glazed over.

"Maybe you're right, but at least I'm honest with myself."

They stared at each other like two prize fighters waiting for the bell to ring.

"Fine. I'll go."

"Good. Go!" Dolores said, as she walked to the door.

"Bitch."

"Fuck you, hater!" Dolores shot back.

Liz gave a final stare as Dolores left the room.

◻◻◻◻

Dolores busted into her suite. Brad was on the bed watching television.

"How'd it go?" Brad looked concerned, reading her body language.

"Not well."

"I told you she was a hater."

"Yeah, I know. I don't know what's wrong with her."

"She's jealous, that's all. And she's a ho."

"She's not a ho, Brad."

"All right. Whatever you say," Brad said, flipping the channels. Dolores watched Brad changing channels without a care in the world. She calmly walked into the bathroom and shut the door. As she turned on the shower, she thought about what she called Liz.

A hater was the last thing Liz was. Liz was the most supportive and loving friend any woman could have. Dolores leaned over the sink and started to cry.

◻◻◻◻

Tony answered his door eagerly, hoping for some good news. He knew it was a long shot, but he wanted to at least talk to Dolores to make sure this was what she really wanted. It was also a final attempt to get the woman he loved. He was not going to get this opportunity again. He wanted to tell her he loved her. And that he wanted to marry her and start a family. Tony felt he had to say these things to have peace of mind.

Liz strolled in, pissed.

"So what she say? Is she going to talk to me?" Tony asked.

Liz threw her hands in the air as if she could careless. "I don't think so. Hell, I don't know."

"Did you get a chance to tell her why I'm here?"

"No, Tony, I didn't. We blew up on each other and that was that."

"Did she say anything?"

"She said she loved him, but I know her better than she knows her damn self. She loves you. Hell, she even said it on accident." A smile appeared on Tony's face. "She called me a hater, and she knows that ain't my style," Liz ranted.

"So what do you think I should do?"

"I don't know. I'm done." Liz sighed. "I was going home, but bump that! I'm going out and get my party on."

"Goin' out?"

"Yeah. Like I said, I'm done. She'll find out who he really is. Fuck her! Gonna call me a hater?" She headed out of the room in a huff.

Tony started to pace the floor, thinking that he had made a mistake coming here. He knew that he left his wife not for Dolores but for himself, and he wanted to tell Dolores that. He also wanted to tell her he loved her. He flopped on the bed, exhausted, staring up at the ceiling.

Tony thought about how hard it was to leave Mary. The woman he had been married to for six years.

ロ ロ ロ ロ

Mary sobbed uncontrollably as Tony told her he was no longer in love with her. "I'm sorry. I can't help how I feel," he said, hating to have to tell her this.

"Is it because of Dolores?"

"No." He sighed. "Mary, let's be honest. Our relationship has run its course."

"Run its course?"

"Yeah."

"That's why your ass was so glad I wasn't pregnant, huh?"

"Look, I'm sorry..."

"Fuck you. You make me sick to my stomach. And don't think you gonna get out of this marriage without paying."

"Whatever. I don't care."

"Oh you will, trust me. You will."

"Look, I just wanna end this as easy as possible so we can go on with our lives."

"I knew I should have gotten pregnant a long time ago."

"Mary, I'm sorry."

"Well, like I said, you will pay."

"Okay, I'll pay. You feel better?" he said, not affected by her threat.

"Did you sleep with her?"

"No." He paused, thinking about Dolores. "But I do think she's my soul mate."

"Soul mate! I'm your soul mate, asshole!" She threw her cell phone at him, hitting him on the head. Tony looked at her blankly, feeling sorry for her.

Tony sat on the edge of the bed in the hotel room, thinking about his next move. "Damn," he said to himself. He grabbed his key card and headed for the door. He was going to fight for the woman he loved. He did not know what he was going to say. But he knew he was going to try to stop her. Tony loved Dolores and he knew she loved him. He felt that he had to give this one last shot.

He ended up at the bar in the lobby, trying to muster the courage he needed to talk to Dolores. He drank until he was too drunk to do anything. And if he did do something, he knew it would be to his own detriment. Suddenly, he heard a familiar voice and turned around. He saw Brad and Dolores walking through the lobby, laughing.

"You are crazy," Dolores said.

"I'm crazy for you," Brad responded.

Tony turned back to the bar, sinking his head between his shoulders.

"I know you are," Dolores replied.

"You better believe it."

"Hey, everybody, I'm crazy about this woman!"

People laughed as Brad made a scene in the lobby. Dolores blushed.

"Yeah, I love him, too," she said, rolling her eyes embarrassed, but laughing.

Tony sat on his stool, frozen. He looked at their reflection in the bar mirror. As they pranced out of the lobby to the pool.

Tony swallowed the lump in his throat. He downed his drink in one gulp and headed back to his room.

ㅁㄱㅁㄱ

The next morning there was a loud knock on the door of Tony's room. Tony woke up still dressed in his clothes from the night before. He was hung over and had a terrible headache.

"Who is it?!"

"It's me."

"Liz?"

"Yeah. Who the hell else could it be?"

Tony stumbled to the door. "What's going on?" he asked.

"I'm leaving."

"I thought you were gonna stay for a while."

"I changed my mind. I'm leaving today," Liz said.

Tony thought about how happy Dolores looked last night. "Cool. We can catch a flight together."

"You not going to try to see her?" Liz asked.

"Nah. I saw her last night."

"You did?"

"I didn't talk to her. She didn't even see me. I was drunk at the bar, and she and Brad walked through the lobby. She looked happy."

"She ain't happy, fool!"

"She looked happy to me."

"Goodbye, Tony." Liz turned to leave.

"Liz?"

"What?"

"Why is it so hard for you to believe she really is in love, and happy?" Tony asked.

"Because I know her. That's why. And most of all I know Brad." Liz turned and walked away.

THIRTY-THREE

Tony finished packing his suitcases and sat on his bed thinking about Dolores. He took out a quarter and set it on his thumb. "Okay. If it lands heads, I'll go home. If it lands tails, I'll tell Dolores I love her and that she's making a terrible mistake." He flipped the coin, caught it, and slapped it on the back of his hand. Tails. "All right, one more time." He flipped the coin and it came up tails again. "Damn. All right, one more time." He flipped it again.

◌ ◌ ◌ ◌

Dolores was in her wedding gown, staring in the mirror. She spun around, admiring her dress. Suddenly a sadness came over her face, but her mother walked in and Dolores quickly smiled.

"Oh, baby, you look beautiful!" her mother said, wearing an even bigger smile.

"Thank you, mom."

"I am so proud of you."

"Thanks, mom."

Her mother noticed something was wrong. She could see it in her daughter's eyes. The eyes of uncertainty. Smiling on the outside but scared on the inside.

"Is something wrong?"

"No. I'm just a little nervous."

"Well don't be. You are a beautiful woman who's about to marry a very wonderful, handsome man."

"Mom, can I ask you something?"

"Sure. What?"

"How did you know dad was the right guy?"

"I just knew. I loved him first and foremost. And I knew he would always take care of me, in every way a woman needs to be taken care of. Most of all, I knew he would take care of my heart."

Dolores smiled.

A woman came in to do her make-up. Dolores gazed happily in the mirror as the make-up artist put the final touches on her face.

A knock on the open door got everyone's attention. "Come in," Dolores shouted.

It was Liz.

Liz gave everyone but Dolores a hug. It was obvious something was wrong. Dolores looked at Liz, not saying a word. Liz smiled at Dolores' reflection in the mirror.

"Hey," Liz said.

"Hey," Dolores replied.

"We gotta talk."

"Liz, let's talk later all right. After the wedding."

"No, we need to talk now."

"C'mon, everybody, let's give them some privacy," Jackie said. Everyone followed Jackie out of the room.

Dolores turned around and stared at Liz. The side of her mouth was twisted up. Liz looked at her with her hands on her hips, ready to go at it.

"Liz, I'm not getting into this now—not before my wedding."

"Am I your friend?"

"What?"

"Am I your friend?" Liz repeated.

"I thought you were."

"I don't know why I'm even talking to you." Liz said and rolled her eyes.

"What, Liz? What's so important that you have to ruin my wedding?"

"Look, I'm not trying to argue, but I feel like I have to tell you this." Liz grabbed a chair. She carried it over to Dolores and sat next to her. "Dolores, I wouldn't be here if I didn't love you. Look, girl, I just need to tell you that Brad is not right for you. He's a dog, and he's no good. Follow your heart. He cheated on you once, he's gonna do it again."

"Are you done?" Dolores asked.

Liz folded her arms, irritated. "Yeah, I'm done."

"Look, I know he cheated on me. But that doesn't give you the right to tell me I can't forgive my fiancé."

"I'm not trying to tell you…"

"Yes you are!"

"If you marry this man, you will be making the biggest mistake of your life…"

There was a knock on the open door. Brad stuck his head inside. He saw Liz and shot her a dirty look. "Is everything all right?" Brad asked Dolores. Liz looked at Brad, disgusted.

"Yeah," Dolores replied.

"Nah, it ain't all right. You need to tell Dolores what you did."

"Dolores, your friend is a hater and a ho. Now come on, let's go get married."

"A coward to the end."

"Fuck you!" Brad snapped. "Now come on, Dolores, let's go!"

"No, fuck you. Now tell her what you did!"

"I don't know what you're talking about."

"Yes you do."

"No I don't."

"You raped me!"

Dolores looked at Brad, stunned, waiting for him to deny it. However, his response was slow. Everyone in the hallway looked inside.

"I didn't rape you. Bitch, you crazy."

"Fuck you," Liz shot back.

Brad looked at Dolores, eyes telling it all.

"I know you don't believe her," Brad said, changing his expression from guilty to innocent. "Look, this bitch is jealous of you, and she's lying."

"Girl, I wanted to tell you. But I was scared to."

"Are you lying?" Dolores asked.

"No. Have you ever known me to lie?"

Dolores looked at Brad, hoping he would have some way to prove he was not capable of such an act.

"I didn't touch you!" Brad snapped. He stomped toward Liz, enraged, and raised his hand.

"Brad!" Dolores screamed, stopping Brad's hand in mid air. Liz just stood there, eyes fixed on him.

"I need to talk to you," Dolores said to Brad.

"What? You believe her?"

"I don't know. You tell me. Should I?"

"Yes, you should," Tony said, as he entered the room.

"What the fuck are you doing here?" Brad said, looking at Tony like he wasn't invited to the party.

"I'm here for a friend," Tony replied.

"Get the fuck out of here!" Brad shouted.

"Fuck you!" Tony shot back. Brad and Tony went for each other, but Dolores stepped between them.

"Stop!!!" Dolores screamed. "Tony, you have to go."

Tony stood there, adrenaline pumping. He looked at Brad, heated.

"Fine. Just talk to your girl. All right?"

"I will. Now go," Dolores said.

Tony looked at Liz and Dolores and walked out. More of Dolores' people gathered outside, looking in to see what the commotion was all about.

"Listen, Dolores," Liz said.

"Dolores, let's just go," Brad chimed in.

"No. I want to hear this."

"But you know what she's trying to do."

"I said I want to hear this!" Dolores gave Liz her full attention.

"Remember last year for my birthday, Brad drove me home cause I had too much to drink?" Dolores looked at her eyes glazed, horrified by the truth that Liz would tell.

〄 〄 〄 〄

Liz stumbled into her apartment, drunk. Brad walked in behind her.

"Thanks for the ride, Brad." Liz gave him a quick hug. He hugged her back then put his hands in his pockets and looked around.

"This is cool. How long have you been living here?"

"About five years. Rent control, so they're going to have to drag me out of here kicking and screaming."

"I heard that." Brad looked around again. "Can I use the bathroom?"

"Yeah, sure." She pointed down the hall. "It's right back there, to the right."

As Brad strolled to the bathroom, Liz went to the kitchen and started to make some coffee.

"You want some coffee?" Liz shouted.

"Nah, I'm cool," Brad shouted back.

Brad walked out of the bathroom wiping his hands with a paper towel. He tossed it in the trash. "All right, I'm gonna go." He stood for a moment taking in his surroundings. He stared at Liz in her tight fitted jeans that showed her voluptuous over sized round ass and thick thighs. His eyes danced up to her blouse where the top three buttons were open, showing off her D-cups. Brad looked like he was having an internal war with himself, as he watched her make coffee. He could see the alcohol having its way with her, making her sway back and forth.

"All right, Brad, thanks for the ride." She walked him to the door.

"Cool. No problem." Brad gave her a hug, but didn't let go. "Damn, you feel good."

Liz looked at him strangely. Brad held her tighter. And although she was drunk, she knew what he was doing was not okay. But he was tipsy, too, so she gave him a pass and laughed it off.

"Brad, what are you doing?"

"Nothing."

"Well, uh, could you like, let me go?" Liz said, looking up at him while her head spun from the alcohol. Brad kept his arms locked around her waist, smiling. "Brad, you're with my girl."

"I know. I just wanna hold you."

Liz turned serious. "Okay, I'm not playing, stop."

"Girl, you know you want me. I see the way you be lookin' at me," Brad said. He tried to kiss Liz, but she pulled back.

"Brad, stop! Stop! You're cute and all, but you're with my girl, and that's where it ends."

"Okay. Just give me one kiss and I'll let you go." He smiled.

She felt Brad's arms around her waist tightly locked. "No."

"Please." She sighed.

"One kiss?"

"Yeah, one kiss," Brad said softly.

She thought for a moment, then gave him a peck on the cheek. "There. Now let me go."

"Girl, that wasn't no real kiss. Now give me a little kiss on the lips," he said with a smile.

"You lucky I'm drunk or I would have kicked you in the balls along time ago."

They both gave a little laugh.

Brad kept his arms locked around her waist. He started to rock her back and forth like a pendulum on a clock, waiting for her to kiss him. She rolled her eyes then gave him a kiss on the lips. He immediately stuck his tongue in her mouth. She tried to pull away again, but he held her tighter. "Okay, you got your kiss. Now let me go. I'm not playing!"

"Neither am I. Now give me another kiss," he said, still wearing a smile trying to be charming.

"What are you, twelve?"

Brad kissed her hard. They began to struggle. Liz finally stopped fighting him, realizing he was too strong.

"C'mon, Brad, why you trippin'?" Liz said, feeling true fear for the first time.

"I'm not trippin'. We're just messing around," he said, still charming.

"Well, fine. Playtime is over now, so let me go."

"Not until you give me a kiss like you mean it."

"I already gave you one. Now stop!"

"Okay, look. One more kiss and I'll leave."

"You're trippin'… what about my girl?"

"I know, it's just, you know how it is. Just give me a kiss like you mean it and I'll let you go. It's okay. It's just a kiss damn." Liz thought about it for a moment, feeling the alcohol turning on her, making her feel queasy.

"You promise you'll leave right after?"

"I promise."

Liz sighed, frustrated. She puckered up. Brad stopped just before their lips touched.

"Like you mean it."

Liz rolled her eyes and their lips met. Brad's tongue slid into Liz's mouth, and her tongue met his. Their kiss lasted a few seconds, then Liz stopped.

"All right, now. That's it. You gotta go," Liz said, staring straight into Brad's eyes so there would be no misunderstanding how she felt. Brad looked at her for a moment, then forced more kisses on her. Liz tried to fight him, but he overpowered her. He picked her up and pinned her against the wall. Liz squirmed and bucked, trying to escape his grasp.

"Mothafucka, let me go!" she shouted.

"Shut up, bitch!" Brad slapped her, knocking her to the floor.

Liz was stunned. For the second time in her life, she knew she was not in control. "What are you doing?" she said in a softer tone.

"Look, I'm not going to hurt you. You know you want me." Brad stared at her with cold eyes and a devilish smirk. He slowly unbuttoned her blouse while keeping a strong grip on Liz's throat. "Dolores won't ever have to know. We'll just do this, this one time, okay?"

"Please don't," Liz said as tears streamed down her face.

"It's okay," Brad said, trying to be as nice as possible. He opened her blouse, exposing her bra. Her breasts were too big for the bra she was wearing. Brad licked his lips and pulled her bra up. He paused for a moment, taking in the beauty of her voluptuous breasts. When Liz tried to move, he tightened his grip around her neck. He unbuttoned her jeans and slowly slid them down past her ankles, then tossed them to the side. He kissed her chest gently, convincing himself that he was making love, not raping her. Liz was flushed, with tears streaming down her face. He then slowly took off her panties. "This never happened," he said, looking deep into her eyes.

Tears poured down Dolores' face as she watched Liz cry. Brad stared at Liz, arms folded with no expression. Family and friends stood in the doorway, flabbergasted.

"Are you done yet?" Brad asked.

"Fuck you!" Liz shouted.

Brad stood there calm and cool. "She's lying," he said. "I know you don't believe her."

Dolores sat there overwhelmed. She looked at Brad for a moment.

"You believe her?" Brad asked. He sounded convincing, but Dolores could see in his eyes he was guilty. She saw the same eyes that lied to her in the shower when she caught him cheating. Suddenly she was like boiling water in a teakettle that could blow at anytime.

"You son of a bitch!" Dolores jumped out of her chair and rushed Brad swinging wildly. Brad blocked her punches, then smacked her across the face. Liz rushed him and jumped on his back, scratching his face. Brad spun around trying to get her off of his back. He finally threw Liz off, sending her to the ground. Dolores swung again. She got in a few licks, but Brad grabbed her by the arms.

"What the fuck is wrong with you!"

He raised his hand to give her another slap, but Tony grabbed it, then followed with a right hook to Brad's jaw. The two of them tussled, knocking furniture all over the place. Tony ended up on top of Brad, whaling on him. Brad was a bloody mess as he took the ass whoopin' of his life. Tony completely lost it, throwing punch after punch.

"Stop, Tony, he's not worth it!" Dolores yelled, pulling Tony off.

Dolores' people stood in shock.

Liz walked over staring down at Brad, halfway unconscious with a bloody mouth and nose. Her eyes were red and full of tears. She kicked Brad's legs open spread eagle. Everyone knew what was to come. In their hearts they wanted to stop her, but they all felt that if a kick in the balls would help her have closure, it would be worth it.

Liz wiped her face and kicked Brad in the nuts. Hard.

Brad screamed in pain.

Liz repeated this form of therapy three more times.

Brad passed out.

"Liz," Dolores said in almost a motherly tone.

Liz stared at Brad helpless, curled up like a baby in the fetal position.

"Liz," she repeated. Dolores walked up to her and hugged her. They sobbed in each other's arms. Tony stood to the side, watching. Family members walked around looking at the broken furniture, and Brad on the floor. Even Rob and Zach, Brad's closest friends, walked in stunned.

Dolores looked at Tony and mouthed "Thank you."

# THIRTY-FOUR

Dolores and Liz sat on the beach that night, looking out at the black sea. They were wrapped in blankets drinking wine.

"I'm so sorry, girl. Why didn't you tell me?" Dolores took a sip out of the wine bottle.

"I don't know. Scared, embarrassed. Guilty," Liz answered, staring out at the ocean, drinking out of her own bottle.

"Guilty for what? He raped you."

"Trust me, I wanted to tell you, but I didn't want you to get mad at me or think that I tried anything on him."

"Girl, I wouldn't have thought that. Liz, you're my best friend."

"Please. You know best friends fall out all the time over men."

"That's true," Dolores agreed. They sat and watched the small waves crash on the beach, enjoying the sound of the water.

"You know, all my life I've felt like I've been searching for the love of a man, trying to find someone who would love me unconditionally. You know?" Liz said.

"I know."

"Someone to tell me I was beautiful, smart, and most of all special, even when I didn't feel like it. Girl, I've had sex with so many men I couldn't count them if I tried... You're a virgin, Dolores, and I admire the hell out of that. I always have."

"Is that why you did what you did at that party in Long Beach?" Dolores asked, leaning on Liz's shoulder.

"I guess. You're like the sister I never had. And I would rather have sex with two guys than see you have someone take something so precious from you. Shit, to me it's just sex, but to you, it means something. I think during these last months I kind of forgot that, and I'm sorry."

"Like my mom always said, "Dolores, you're the first example of how people should treat you." I guess it kind of stuck."

"Yeah, for thirty-two years."

They gave a little laugh.

"I didn't know it would stick that damn long."

"Well it did. And now you get to make love for the first time with your future husband. And how many women get to say that?" Liz said, truly happy for her.

"Not enough, unfortunately." Dolores sighed. "But I do want you to know, back when we were in college and we were out in Long Beach, and we were both drunk, and so were those two guys. And that guy started to get rough with me, and didn't believe that I was a virgin. I mean, he was going to rape me…"

"Dolores, you don't…"

"I know. I just want you know. I was drunk, but I wasn't that drunk. Those guys were on a whole other level. And when he had me pinned down. And you stopped him. By doing what you did, I just couldn't understand why someone would do that for another person. I mean, I wouldn't have done that for you. You're an amazing person, Liz. It's like you saved my life twice. My personal guardian angel."

Liz smiled, touched. "I love you, too." Liz kissed the top of Dolores' head. She felt prouder of that act of friendship than anything she'd ever done in her life. "I'm so happy for you."

"Thank you. So, how did you know I loved Tony?" Dolores asked.

Liz thought about it for a nice moment. "We're best friends, remember?" They continued to stare at the water with Dolores' head resting on Liz's bosom. "So where is Tony?" Liz asked.

"Back at his room. We're gonna meet for breakfast tomorrow. I told him tonight I wanted to be with my best friend."

"Good." Liz smiled.

卍 卍 卍 卍

Tony strolled to the front door of his hotel room. "Who is it?" he asked.

"It's me."

Tony answered the door. "Hey."

"Hey," Dolores said with a smile. She looked beautiful in a sundress, with her hair pulled back. Tony led her to a breakfast spread by the balcony. "Wow, the food's here already."

"Yeah, just got here," Tony replied.

"It's good to see you."

Dolores and Tony gave each other a quick hug. They smiled, showing a little nervousness.

"I ain't gonna front. I've been thinking about you all night," Tony said.

"You have?"

"Yeah, I thought I lost you. I mean, we were all set to get on that plane, but then Liz told me what he did." They stared at each other, hearts pounding. Dolores hugged Tony and they embraced again, this time not letting go.

"I love you."

Dolores' words made him smile. "You sure?" Tony asked.

"Yeah."

Tony stared into her eyes for a long moment. "I love you too."

Dolores smiled. "Can I see something?" she asked.

"What?"

"Shh," Dolores said, her eyes seeming to look through him. She put her hands on the sides of his face, then gently kissed him. Tony smiled. They both felt magic between them. "I knew it," Dolores said. Their eyes locked. "You feel that?"

"Yeah," Tony replied.

"It feels right, don't it?" Dolores said, tickled by the way her body tingled inside.

"Yeah, it does," Tony answered.

Dolores' eyes watered up and a tear fell. Tony wiped the tear away, then kissed her passionately. They both were beaming.

"Look, Tony, let's just take it slow. Okay?"

"Sounds good to me. Hey, I got a surprise for you."

"What?" Dolores asked.

"I'm not gonna tell you."

"Why not?" Dolores persisted.

"Because it's a surprise. I'll tell you in a few weeks."

"Whatever, man." Dolores kissed him again.

 **THIRTY-FIVE**

Dolores was working hard at her desk when the phone rang. It was Liz. They talked about the latest drama in Liz's life. Dolores talked about how she had been talking to Tony on the phone every night until three in the morning. She told Liz how their relationship had grown, and how she really believed that everything that happened, happened for a reason. She talked about how Tony was the best thing that ever happened to her, and how she planned to move back to LA in a year, and they would probably get engaged then. Liz listened, smiling, stifling a laugh as Dolores rambled on about her plans. Liz knew something she didn't.

They talked about how good God is, and how they couldn't wait for Liz to come out to New York and hang. Dolores told Liz that she was the bravest, best friend a girl could have, and that she appreciated her for what she called saving her life. This brought a huge smile to Liz's face. A short while later they said that they loved one another and hung up the phone.

Dolores looked happy, even though she was exhausted from all the late-night conversations with Tony. She yawned and got up, mesmerized by the beautiful city lights. She felt like she was living in a whole new world. Suddenly a sadness came over her but just as quickly a smile took over. Dolores walked down the hall to the coffee room. As she poured herself a cup of coffee, Tony appeared behind her, looking suave.

"Can I get some of that?" Tony asked.

"Sure, go right..." Her eyes sprang wide open with shock. "Oh my God! What are you doin' here?" They embraced.

"I just thought I'd come out here and take you out."

"Yeah, right. Why are you really out here?"

Tony stared at her for a nice moment, not saying a word. "What?" she asked, confused by his silence. Tony smiled.

"I talked to Bently about transferring me out here, because of course with my asthma, I can't really handle the smog in L.A. So I called Bob and asked him if he was interested in coming back to L.A. and trading jobs. He couldn't wait. Bently approved it, so here I am." Dolores' emotions started to overwhelm her. She gave Tony another hug. Their faces were flushed with happiness. "Like my surprise?"

"Yeah." She thought for a moment, "but the smog is worse out here."

"But it's a different kind of smog. I googled it. It's better for me out here."

"Is that right?" They laughed.

"Yep. So I will pick you up tonight to celebrate."

"How do you know I'm not busy?"

"Well, are you?" Tony smiled.

"Well, I guess I can break my other plans."

"You better."

Dolores' art deco home was beautiful. The doorbell rang and Dolores strolled to the front door dressed to kill. She wore a long black gown that showed off every curve imaginable. She looked gorgeous. She opened the door and Tony stood there holding a single red rose, dressed to the tee. "Hey," he said amazed by her beauty.

"Hey."

Tony drove Dolores' Lexus while Dolores sat in the passenger seat. They were quiet, glancing at each other adoringly. They eventually came to a red light and stopped. Tony looked like he wanted to say something. He looked in his rearview mirror to see if any cars were coming. There were none.

They gazed into each other's eyes. They kissed passionately. Tony suddenly stopped. "Wait. Let's take it slow," Tony said.

"Okay," Dolores said, not wanting to.

"Okay, Dolores, will you marry me?" The words leaped from his mouth, as if he were going to lose his mind if he didn't get them out. He eased out a black velvet box and opened it. The diamond ring was huge, at least six carats. Dolores' eyes welled up. Tony realized that he messed up the whole night he had planned for her. "I'm sorry I said it now. I just couldn't hold it in any longer. I had everything planned—violins and flowers at this great restaurant—but I just couldn't hold it in…"

Dolores attacked Tony passionately kissing him. As they kissed, drivers behind them honked their horns and pulled around them shouting obscenities.

Tony pulled the car over to the side of the dark road, and they continued to make out.

"Dolores, I love you so much."

"I love you, too."

"So?" Tony asked.

"Of course I'll marry you." They kissed passionately. Tony's hands roamed Dolores' body as he kissed her harder and harder. Dolores grabbed his hand putting it between her legs.

"Hey," Tony said, snatching his hand back.

"Oh yeah, I'm sorry. My bad," Dolores said, amused. They both laughed their asses off.

"Don't start nothing you can't finish," Tony said, still laughing.

# THIRTY-SIX

A beautiful church wedding was in progress. Tony and Dolores were at the altar reciting their vows. Liz was her maid of honor; Dolores' cousin Carrie stood next to Liz as one of the bridesmaids.

The parents looked on, proud. Tony and Dolores kissed and family and friends cheered. They hopped over a broom, signifying marriage in African-American culture, and strolled down the aisle. Liz leaned over to Carrie.

"Girlfriend earned that white dress," Liz said, swollen with pride.

"Who you tellin'?" Carrie responded, wearing a huge smile.

🔲 🔲 🔲 🔲

That night Tony lay in bed waiting. Dolores stepped out of the bathroom wearing a sexy nightgown, showing plenty of cleavage and legs. Her beautiful brown skin glistened from head to toe. Tony's eyes opened wide. She strolled toward him and straddled him. They kissed passionately.

Dolores was ready.

As Tony slowly took off her gown, she felt a feeling she had never felt before, and knew she would never feel again. To make love for the first time, with the man she shared vows with.

Tony maneuvered on top of her as they continued to kiss. Then his face suddenly went blank.

"What's wrong?" Dolores asked.

Tony peeped under the covers. "Uh, I think I might be a little too excited." Tony's look of confusion turned into a big smile. "Oh, never mind."

Dolores sighed with relief.

Tony kissed her passionately, then adjusted himself for lovemaking. He could feel Dolores' belly tremble in anticipation of what was to come. She licked her lips, uncontrollably, feeling like her tongue needed some place to go. He sucked her nipples, biting the tips just hard enough to make her core tremble. She bit his shoulder hard, wanting him to enter her and put out the flame that was burning inside. She squeezed his penis hard, now knowing where all the blood in his body must have been. She loved his mind, and she loved his body—most of all she loved his rock-hard penis that made her feel like she was the luckiest woman alive. He was hers and she was his. And nothing could destroy the love that these two now shared as they consummated their marriage.

"Hmmmmmmmmm," they both moaned.

Tony kissed her long and hard, forcing himself deeper and deeper inside her. Dolores' eyes rolled back into her head as she began to get into the throes of lovemaking. She was a virgin no longer, and their bond was sealed.

That night they did everything for each other, and to each other. Dolores climaxed over and over, and so did Tony. Smiles and giggles filled their room. Their hearts were in sync, excited about their new life together. Their love was official. Tears streamed down Dolores' face.

"What's wrong?" Tony asked.

"You were worth the wait."

THE END

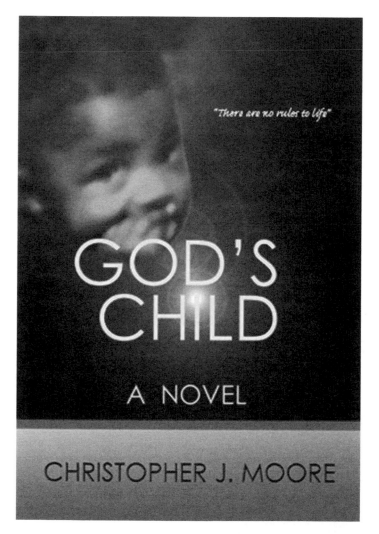

"There are no rules to life"

GOD'S CHILD

A NOVEL

CHRISTOPHER J. MOORE

Visit our website at http://www.clairvoyantbooks.com